Don't Get Mad, Get even

Tom Coffey

To Mary, who else?

First published in 1996 by
Marino Books
An imprint of Mercier Press
16 Hume Street Dublin 2

Trade enquiries to Mercier Press
PO Box 5, 5 French Church Street,
Cork

A Marino Original
© Tom Coffey 1996

ISBN 1 86023 040 7

10 9 8 7 6 5 4 3 2 1

A CIP record for this title is available
from the British Library

Cover design by
Adrienne Geoghegan
Set by Richard Parfrey in Caslon
Regular 9.5/15
Printed in Ireland by ColourBooks,
Baldoyle Industrial Estate, Dublin 13.

The Publishers acknowledge with
gratitude the financial assistance of The
Arts Council/An Chomhairle Ealaíon.

ONE

Any man who has suffered the pangs of unrequited sex will readily agree that it shouldn't happen to a dog. But to be super-abundantly endowed in that particular quarter, and still no takers, shouldn't happen even to a dirty dog like Harry Skelly. Yet happen it did, which is why the wiring under the assembly lines was in constant need of maintenance.

And there, sure enough, was the decent man himself on diligent hands and knees underneath line three and he armed to the teeth with customary screwdriver, pliers and burning carnal urge. Along by Harry's left flank ran the narrow, vinyl-tiled walkway between assembly lines two and three, while to his right there stretched a colonnade of feminine legs as palatable as ever whetted a man's appetite. Twenty-four matched pairs all told and all in keen competition for his undivided attention.

Harry was a fully qualified, card-carrying electrician and, in the pursuit of his calling, he had come to know every female knee on the payroll of Worldwide Electronics (Ireland) Ltd; his current mission was to check out the underbench wiring and the new pair of knees just released from the training centre.

Topside of the workbench the unwary owners of those provocative props were in labour bringing forth their daily brood of Model K radios, the Company's pride and joy and main source of bread. With that monotonous ambidexterity at which women have few equals, one hundred and thirty-two

3

nimble fingers and forty-eight thumbs fed their quotas of electronic entrails to the procession of printed circuit boards on the moving belt. And, as they sang along with the productively piped music, not a single vibe of that much-vaunted feminine intuition gave warning of the danger that lurked among their nethers.

Cautiously, Harry skirted around the black stockings with the exceptionally fast reflexes; disdainfully he cut dead the white pair that felt like canvas bags filled with jelly; furtively he dogtrotted past the exposed space where the knife-edged shins were out sick and, there before him, invitingly rounded and accessibly short-skirted, rose the twin objects of his quest.

He moved smoothly within easy groping range and rolled over on hip and elbow for a preliminary survey.

The view before him was pleasant indeed, with contours as appealing as ever put bad thoughts in a man's mind, and a tingle of anticipation ran through Harry's fingertips and other places too numerous or delicate to mention.

He paused to verify that his head and other vital equipment were beyond the range of those solid brown shoes, then he reached out a tentative forefinger to touch the reflex button just below the near knee.

He felt the limb give forth a tremor, barely perceptible, and that was all. Wary of delayed reflexes, he waited a moment and, when nothing untoward happened, he pressed again with more emphasis. Still the shoes maintained their non-aggressive alignment and Harry's hopes etcetera began to rise noticeably. Abandoning further preliminaries, he engulfed the knee in his hairy fist and squeezed. Still the limb remained passive and the shoe wavered not.

Rarely indeed did Harry progress this far unmolested and, understandably, his approach began to lose some of its objectivity. Now, acting more or less on their own initiative, his fingers took off at an excited trot in a northerly direction, never hesitating until they reached the point where the hosiery grew thicker for that extra confidence. With the blood now also pounding fiercely in his ears, the fingers performed a nimble sidestep towards front and centre.

Up above, the girl's face betrayed no sign of what was going on in her mind or beneath her skirt. Her task was to cover up blemishes on the passing circuit boards with artistic little daubs of solder. They called it product enhancement, no less, and it called for a keen eye, a steady hand and close concentration. It was her first day on the line and she had no wish to attract any untoward attention. But, as the seconds passed, a close observer might have noted that her concentration was beginning to wander, her breathing a little faster and her eyelids fluttering more rapidly than normal. Then, suddenly, without warning, her self-control crashed. Quickly, furtively, she reached under the bench and began to stroke the back of Harry's hand with a red-hot soldering iron.

The message that his hand was being systematically sautéd took some time to reach Harry's brain, probably because of the more pressing signals emanating from his genitals. But finally, he began to suspect that all was not well and, with great reluctance, he withdrew the hand for inspection. With more than passing interest, he examined the pink blisters now beginning to emerge through the thick hair on his hand.

'Mother of Jaw-sus!' Harry remarked softly but with sincerity.

In his many years of underbench exploration Harry had suffered more than his share of punishment. He had been kneed about the head to the point of concussion. He had been raked with nailfiles and acupunctured with steel combs. When fashion had so ordained, he had been stiletto-heeled in the anus. But never in the history of his endeavour had he been barbecued with a soldering iron. The indignity of it hurt him to the quick. The hand didn't feel so good either.

'Jaw-sus!' said he once more, this time giving full vent to his powerful lungs.

5

Harry's anguished bellow did not go unnoticed and, almost immediately, an outbreak of sideways-tilted faces appeared among the knees.

"Tis Horny Harry!' a high-frequency voice cried out and suddenly the air was shredded by screams for blood while every shoe within flailing distance set upon the defenceless man with great abandon and fair accuracy.

It took several savage kicks to the head to bring Harry to the conclusion that evasive action was called for. Then, howling like a banshee, he rolled out into the aisle.

The sounds of strife brought Andy Sexton on the scene at a ladylike canter and the sight that met his limpid eyes brought him screeching to a halt.

There was Horny Harry laid out on the floor, streaming blood and loud profanity. There was Andy's production crew, with bosoms hazardously pendant above the moving belt, the better to hurl abuse at their victim. Worst of all, there was the procession of mottled green boards gliding by on the line, unheeded and unfed.

'What the feck is going on?' Andy shrieked.

'Ye bloody pack of looneys,' Harry roared at the girls, ignoring the interruption.

'He was gropin' again,' a girl informed Andy. 'The dirty oul' hoor's ghost!' she added for good measure.

Andy gazed sadly on the lengthening train of unstuffed circuit boards and he knew that when Quality Control got their talons on that lot he was in the mire, but good. Fiercely, he turned on Harry.

'Shag off ourra here, you!' he piped.

'And who'll fix the wiring?' enquired Harry, blowing forcefully on his newly acquired blisters.

Andy cast a practised eye along the assembly line. Solder fumes hung like morning fog in the air, just out of reach of the extractor fans. The moving belt gave forth an anguished squeal. The neon lights flickered disorientingly. The heady aroma from the hot epoxy pinched viciously at the nostrils. All looked well.

'What's up with the wiring?' he demanded.

'Sure, isn't that what I was trying to find out,' Harry pointed out reasonably, 'when them screamin' biddies tried to kick the shaggin' head offa me.'

'There's nothing wrong with my line,' Andy insisted.

'Comereta me,' Harry tucked the hand for solace between his loins, 'didn't ya ever hear of preventive maintenance?'

Andy knew that by now his day's production was irretrievably blown, and he lost his cool.

'You feck off ourra here,' he screamed at the top of his little lungs, 'and prevent something else.'

Harry uncoiled his six foot three of skin and hair off the floor and looked disdainfully down on Andy's lissom five-six.

'Go 'way,' said he with contempt, 'ya little sparrafart.'

Andy began to dance with rage and frustration.

'Feck off,' he screamed, 'feck off ourra that!'

'Rule seventeen!' thundered Harry, and the change of topic gave Andy pause.

'What are you talking about?' he enquired shrilly.

'Rule seven-bloody-teen. No indecent or profane language allowed in the factory.'

'Who's using indecent or profane language?' Andy demanded.

'You are!'

'No I amn't!'

'Didn't ya tell me to feck off, didn't ya?'

'Feck off isn't indecent or profane!'

'It feckin' well is,' Harry affirmed. 'And you'll be hearing from my feckin' Union about it.'

And with those ominous words on his lips, Harry took himself off to the Medical Centre to have his wounds dressed and, hopefully, get to close quarters with the dimpled knees of the plant nurse.

Frantically Andy set about trying to soothe his girls. He

7

promised them a modesty curtain along the front of the bench, barbed wire fences around their chairs, an operation for Harry. Anything if they would only try to salvage some remnants of the day's production schedule.

Brian A. Collins, Personnel and Training Manager. So says the dymo-printed strip on the office door. Inside, seated at his desk, is the man himself. Crumpled in the middle like an understuffed teddy bear. Heels resting surreptitiously on an open lower drawer. Hands hanging limply over the sides of his bucket chair. Head bowed forward and a fist-sized clump of ginger-blond hair hanging down over his forehead. Take note. He may well become our leading character.

Despite appearances, Collins is not sleeping on Company time. For the hourly-paid workers on the floor Company time begins at eight thirty but their more delicate, salaried colleagues do not assume their duties until nine, and the digital clock on the desk shows eight fifty. Besides, Collins is not actually asleep. The fact is that he is big into meditation and so, each morning before facing the tribulations of the day, he disconnects his internal circuitry for fifteen minutes of deep relaxation. He hasn't yet figured out what good it does but it is bound to improve him in some way, and Collins is a glutton for self-improvement.

At eight fifty-five, on cue, the digital clock sends out a couple of discreet beeps. Company time is about to set in.

Collins surfaces quickly and shifts over to his isometric exercises. His fitted, white-on-white shirt takes the strain of a well-cared-for set of muscles plus just a little excess lard around his solar plexus.

– *Three years this month* –

He pushes his knees upward against the underside of the desk, at the same time pressing down hard with his palms on its top. And, as he punishes his muscles to the maximum, he finds himself taking personal stock.

Just three years since he abandoned an unpromising teaching career in Dublin and, at the age of thirty, ventured out into the real world.

 – *Now look at you with your two-window office the engineers accountants supervisors are all stuck in little one-window cells or packed into communal compounds with no windows at all . . . double the salary of a teacher . . . and Lucy, lovely Lucy, pregnant – at last. –*

The culmination of five years of determined and pleasurable efforts.

 – *And best of all – yeah – back at home. –*

Enough good things in fact to bring pangs of remorse to the soul of even the most hardened survivor of a guilt-edged Catholic upbringing.

 – NINE O'CLOCK! GET CRACKING NOW! –

He bends sideways and pulls his 'pending' file from the lower desk drawer and, as he does, the letter in his hip pocket rustles ominously, reminding him of the one dark cloud on his horizon.

Collins's pending file is a model of simple efficiency. The green folder is divided into three sections, one tagged 'urgent', one 'important' and the third 'urgent and important'. First thing every morning he juggles with the contents and when an 'important' or an 'urgent' moves into the 'urgent and important' section, it is time to go into action. Over the years, he has learned another valuable lesson; given enough time, many of the important items become less important while the urgent ones often take care of themselves.

Today, top of the urgent and important pile is a yellow Post-it slip with a printed heading:

Memo:

From the desk of Mervyn P. Andrews

This item is both urgent and important because Mervyn P. happens to be Collins's immediate boss.

The handwritten message is brief and to the point: 'Brian, please comply with the attached c.c. to me.'

9

The attachment, all the way from Corporate headquarters in Philadelphia, is something else.

Memo
From: B. B. Jackson, Manager, Affirmative Action,
To: M. P. Andrews, Irish Subsidiary:

Merv
We are currently preparing a major report on our Company-wide performance against our Affirmative Action goals. Please, therefore, let me have a breakdown of minorities on your current payroll under the following headings: Blacks, Hispanics, American Indians, Females, Vietnam Veterans, Handicapped.

Please note that where an individual employee may fit into more than one category, you should count him or her separately in all relevant categories.

This report should be submitted to me on a monthly basis to reach this office by the second working day following month end.

Thank you for your cooperation.

B. B. J.

– Oh, shit –
The little voice inside his head always speaks in italics and it has little regard for the conventions of punctuation.
– Blacks or Indians or Vietnam veterans around here! Are they out of their bloody minds! Another of their numbers games –
A banshee howl floats in on the air and he has a foreboding that it will end up on the other side of his desk.
– What about Angela Martin? Now couldn't the name Martin be Hispanic if you put the accent on the last syllable and hasn't she a bit of a limp since she fell off her bicycle; that's female Hispanic and handicapped three minorities rolled into one . . . three brownie points mustn't say brownie points they'd probably

10

consider that a racist remark –

He is right about the banshee. Still howling, Andy Sexton appears before him, prancing with great verve and bringing with him the fire and brimstone fumes from the production floor.

– *Will you just look at the little gobshite –*

– WATCH YOUR LANGUAGE! –

'How's she cutting, Andy?' Collins asks, hoping to exert a calming influence, but Andy is absorbed in his inarticulate frenzy. Several minutes pass before Collins manages to make out a few intelligible words.

'I want that bastard's head!'

'Harry?' Collins enquires superfluously.

'I amn't talking about John the Baptist.'

'What's he up to now?' Collins asked.

'"Up to" is right! All the way up, with one of the new girls.' Without missing a beat in his dance routine, Andy uses his little fists to drum out a tattoo on the sides of his head.

'For the love and honour of God, will you get that bollix out of here!'

'Andy, you know we have to follow the disciplinary procedure,' Collins reasons.

'Disciplinary procedure, my left feckin' testicle.' Andy is a man much given to profane and indecent language except in the presence of his widowed mother or a clerical collar. 'My girls are threatening a feckin' walk-out, so they are.'

This remark gets Collins's full attention.

'They can't do that,' he protests and Andy realises that he is holding a trump card.

'They can, and they will!' he informs Collins and everyone else within loud-hailing range. 'And why wouldn't they? Isn't their virginity at stake?'

Collins decides to let that one pass.

'According to the disciplinary procedure he has to get a written warning,' he reasons.

11

'Didn't he get one of them last month, and what feckin' good did it do?'

Collins shakes his head.

'I know. Tell the girls you're going to give him a second warning this time.'

'Not me,' Andy tells him. 'I amn't his feckin' supervisor.'

Andy is procedurally correct. The warning will have to come from Foley, the Maintenance supervisor.

'All right,' he concedes, 'I'll get Foley to issue it.'

This is another problem, and they both know it.

'That chicken-livered gobshite,' Andy bawls, 'the day *he* issues a written warning, there'll be green blackbirds.'

'Trust me,' says Collins with a confidence that the inside Collins doesn't share. 'Harry will get the warning before the day is out.'

'Take him to the vet. The only way to put a stop to that fella's gallop is to get him dehorned.'

'Just tell the girls not to do anything hasty. I'll take care of the warning.'

Andy's dance has now diminished to an agitated shuffle.

'All right,' he says grudgingly, 'but I better be able to show them a copy of the warning before they go home tonight. Signed by Foley. No, signed by Foley *and* you.'

And with that, off he trots to try to mollify his crew with further dire predictions regarding Harry's fate.

– *Oh, holy Mother of Jesus* –

– LESS OF THAT SWEARING, BOY! –

This is the other voice in his head. It always speaks in strong capitals and is heavily into exclamation marks. Collins recognises that he is now faced with a situation both important and urgent. Also, knowing Harry, one that is fraught with personal danger.

He looks thoughtfully through the half-open and only

slightly dusty venetian blinds. The mountains seem translucent and far away, a sure sign that the good weather will continue. On the green patch in front of the factory a flock of seagulls is beginning to convene. The gulls only venture this far inland when bad weather is on the way, so giving the lie to those too-innocent-looking mountains. The dozen or so birds on the ground are silent, while their friends in the air are raucously argumentative.

Collins begins to pace the space between his desk and the awful painting on the wall, eyes cast downward in thought. He is not a quick thinker and he knows it. All through his schooldays, he was known to be slow in coming up with answers, though it often happened that the answers, when they came, were well-reasoned.

As he paces the office, four steps in each direction, the letter in his pocket rustles again. Another 'urgent, important and possibly hazardous'. He turns aside to his desk and takes the pad of pre-printed warning notices from the top right-hand drawer. Green for first warning, yellow for a second and bright pink for third or final. Three copies to a set. One for the offender, one for his supervisor and one for the Personnel file. On a yellow set, he writes Harry's name and, in the space provided for describing the offence, he enters the words 'sexual harassment' in block letters. Then he takes his suit jacket from its hanger on the back of the door, puts it on, straightens his grey Windsor-knotted tie, draws a deep breath and goes forth to do battle.

Malone could feel one of his bouts of depression coming on. Without too much difficulty, he tore his attention from the week's production report and gazed around the office. His slightly hung-over eye shimmered over the steel-topped desks of his fellow inmates, six in all, each measuring the standard 12.5 square feet and lined up in two neat rows of three. They called it the Engineering Office because, within its prison-grey walls, windowless and paper-thin, they tried to contain the engineers. Here, hemmed in by carefully posed photographs of Company products and labyrinthine circuit diagrams, they fiddled all day long, merrily, with their little scientific calculating machines and dispensed unsolicited advice on how the other departments should be run and weren't.

In short, they engineered.

What bothered Malone most was the absence of windows; the deprivation of daylight; the sense of being cut off from the world of reality. Back home in Cork the warm June sun would surely be shining. The hills would be psychedelically cloaked in glowing yellow furze and purple heather. The soft, sandy beaches would be adorned with undress in various stages of girl and Noreen O'Donnell, who worked in the Co-Op, would be busting out of her blouse with healthy femality. If she could see him now, with his expensive suit and his engineering degree, driving his new red Saab, she might overlook his shortness of stature and allow herself to be cajoled into McCarthy's haybarn on a warm evening. Once there, and in a horizontal position, his height disadvantage would be cancelled out. He wondered for a moment if there was something precocious about being a dirty old man at the age of twenty-five.

Above Malone's head the ventilation system, which occasionally worked, gave forth an agonised moan, ushered in a fresh cloud of heady fumes from the production floor and shattered his pipe dreams into smithereens.

He looked around in search of a bendable ear and went and half-assed himself on a corner of King's desk.

'Jesus,' Malone enquired in hollow tones, 'what's a nice guy like me doing in a dump like this?'

'Not very much,' King conceded without raising his head.

But Malone's need for human intercourse was great and the hint passed by him unheeded. Besides, King happened

14

to be his closest friend, even though he didn't really like the guy all that much.

'Is this all there is to life?' Malone asked dolefully. 'Every bloody day the same. Up at nine. At work by ten past. Off at five. Pissed by seven.'

King sighed and tried to avoid any encouraging eye contact. He'd heard all this before. Many times.

'Smothered by regulations,' Malone went on, undaunted, 'policies and procedures coming out our asses. The system rules! The shaggin' system,' he was now waxing almost oratorical, 'it has us by the short and curlies.' He reached out and grabbed the small disk on King's desktop. Yellow plastic on one side, a black, magnetic coating on the other.

'See what I mean,' Malone complained, holding up the disk.

For want of something useful to do, some well-meaning, underemployed executive in Philadelphia had taken to printing words of Corporate wisdom on these magnetised disks and disseminating them throughout the organisation for the edification and entertainment of all ranks.

In a sombre voice, Malone read out the latest message:

MAN'S GREATEST ADVANTAGE
OVER MACHINE IS
CREATIVITY.
THINK CREATIVE!!

'How the hell do they dream them up?' he asked in awe. 'It can't be easy,' King concurred.

Malone took aim at a fly on the wall and tossed the disk. The fly took evasive action just in time and the disk attached itself to the steel panelling.

'I suppose,' King remarked philosophically, 'it keeps them off the streets.'

King removed his slightly tinted, steel-rimmed spectacles and began to polish them with the end of his sweater.

15

'On the other hand,' he said, gazing myopically into space, 'maybe they have a point.'

'We're not *supposed* to be creative. The system doesn't *allow* us to be creative.'

'Wrong!' said King. 'The system *challenges* us to be creative.'

'Challenge! What bloody challenge?'

'The challenge of beating the system. That's where real creativity comes in. Wait now,' King addressed the ceiling, or possibly Heaven, ' I feel a creative spasm coming on,' he announced. 'I'm about to create a person.'

'It was always my impression,' said Malone, 'that that takes two people. One of each gender, like.'

'Watch me,' King said.

'A bisexual contortionist, by God.'

King picked up his telephone and dialled Anita Merry at Reception.

'Anita, sweetheart,' he asked, 'would you ever mind paging Ignatius Freely for me?'

'Call whom?' enquired Anita, showing off her Leaving Certificate Honours English.

'Ignatius Freely,' King repeated. 'Will you tell him I need to talk to him before he goes home this evening.'

'Right you are, Willie.'

'May you rear a bishop.' King hung up and slipped on that superior expression that Malone found so irritating.

'Wait.' King held up his hand again for silence, and they listened as Anita's modulated tones rang out far and wide on the public address system.

'Will Ignatius Freely please call Reception,' she sang. 'Ignatius Freely call Reception, please.'

'My creation,' King claimed proudly. 'All my own work.'

Malone emerged from his cloud of depression as he began to recognise the possibilities.

'Hey,' he asked, 'can I play?'

'Be my guest.'

16

Malone dialled the print room and a crisp female voice answered.

'Reproduction room,' said the voice. 'Assumpta Kelly speaking.'

'Assumpta,' Malone enquired, 'I was wondering if you might need some help.'

'What kind of help?'

'Well,' said Malone, 'I happen to have some very well-maintained reproductive equipment.'

'Who's speaking?' Assumpta was cautious. Once she had told the Engineering Director to bugger off, thinking it was Malone.

'Malone here.'

'Bugger off!' said Assumpta.

'Hold on a minute,' Malone sensed that she was about to slam the receiver down on his ear. 'We need to add a new name to the management circulation list.'

'All right,' she grumbled, 'wait till I get a Biro.'

Malone turned to King.

'How about a middle initial?' he asked.

'Make it P for Patrick,' King suggested. 'That'll look good on the circulation list – I.P. Freely.'

Assumpta came back on the line.

'All right,' she announced. 'I'm ready.'

'Me too,' Malone responded. 'Open all zippers and I'll be right there.'

Assumpta really liked Malone. So he was only five foot seven in his platform shoes. Still and all, wasn't he dark and handsome and, for her, small men were more sexually arousing. However, she had long ago grown weary of Malone's improper suggestions, because he never showed any inclination to follow up on them. She wasn't to know that the inclination was there in full strength but that whenever Malone came face to face with a nubile female – or face to chest in the case of a well constructed specimen like Assumpta – he was transformed instantly into a craven coward.

'What's the name?' she snapped.

'Ignatius P. Freely.'

'You must be joking!'

'Sure we all have our crosses to bear.'

'All right,' she sighed. 'How do you spell it?'

As Malone spelled the name, Anita's voice rang out again, with a slightly impatient tint, inviting Ignatius please to communicate with her.

'Did you say "B" or "T" for the middle initial?' Assumpta enquired.

'No, it's "P"' said Malone, 'as in toilet.' He hung up the phone and looked earnestly at King. 'I wonder,' he asked, 'if we could get our Ignatius on to the payroll?'

'Let me give it some thought.'

'Jesus,' Malone laughed, 'wouldn't that be something. Wouldn't that put a hair up the system's ass.'

Then the factory hooter screamed at them to go eat and they obeyed without hesitation.

18

Two

– You and your big mouth! –

The little voice was really giving him a hard time.

– You should never have told her in the first place –

And that was the truth. He should have known better than to tell Lucy about the phone call.

The professionally friendly voice on the telephone had started out by asking Collins if he was alone and could he speak freely. Collins, mystified and cautious, closed his office door and said yes. The voice then informed him that it represented a major American electronics company about to start up in the Dublin area and would he be interested in the job of Personnel Director.

– Back to Dublin? No way, Jose! –

But Collins, hampered by his ingrained politeness and pleased that he had been singled out by a headhunter, told the caller that he'd think about it.

The big mistake, as the little voice relentlessly pointed out, had been to tell Lucy about it. Dublin was her world. Dublin was where the action and the culture, at least as a Dubliner would define it, happened to be. Her enthusiasm and excitement at the prospect of returning to her favourite haunts had rolled right over Collins's reservations, which he was smart enough not to voice too strongly at the time anyway.

– You could have screwed up the interview you could have turned them off oh no not you Killer Collins –

And now there was the letter in his hip pocket.

– Haven't you taken enough punishment for one day –

That was true enough. He had spent a frustrating half-hour searching for Harry's supervisor before he found that the guy had gone home with a toothache, doubtless brought on by a foreboding about the warning notice. He had followed up with a search, also in vain, for Harry himself and had then endured a harrowing ninety minutes trying to calm Andy and his girls with promises that Harry would get the yellow card first thing on Monday morning.

– So just keep your mouth shut –

Collins always enjoyed this walk along the Cosaun, a mile and a half, between the plant and his home. The narrow pathway, dusty or muddy depending on the elements, elbowing its way between high hedges of fuchsia, drew out the stresses of the day like a warm poultice. The seagulls had been wrong in their earlier forecast, apart from a brief downpour during lunch break, and now the slanting sun was dimpling the mountains, highlighting folds and creases that were often ironed out under the pale morning light. The wild woodbine hidden in the hedges was revelling in the recent rain and flooding the air with its delicate perfume, strong enough even to subdue the smell of the silage from Kelly's farm on the hill.

– This is your scene, boy. Twelve years at the Christian Brothers down below marks of the leather on your wrists and on your backside sometimes didn't do you any harm either convent girls parading themselves around the street at lunchtime in those awful brown uniforms that left everything to the imagination . . . the real friends . . . and the real enemies too . . . the street football leagues Frank and yourself playing for the Parnells . . . and all the fights that you never wanted to get into and you always won well except one and that didn't count because it was a girl and you couldn't be expected to fight a girl so you ran away when she came at you screaming with her nails all set to scratch your eyes out . . . Lily or Millie or something a big mountainy girl out to slaughter you for beating the shit out of her young brother and he

20

nearly two years older than you. Killer Collins –

He gave a friendly nod to the two pigeons perched, intimately as usual, on the telephone wire. They answered with seductive chuckles. All was right in their world too.

– Who'd want to move back to Dublin? –

Maisie O'Dwyer came around the corner from Parnell Street on to the Cosaun – *Maisie Neligan now* – with her two little girls, one hanging on to each hand. Maisie's mother used to help in the shop after his father had the stroke and sometimes she brought Maisie along with her and let her play in Collins's back garden.

– She remembers –

'Hi, Maisie.'

'Hello, Brian.'

He smiled and waved at the kids. One of them smiled back at him. She bore a strong resemblance to Maisie at that age, but not quite as skinny.

And they were gone past.

– Ah, it was years ago. She's forgotten the whole thing –

But Collins hadn't forgotten.

– There she lay . . .

Yes, there she lay in the back garden sunning herself on the canvas deckchair with the red and white stripes on it wearing a bright yellow dress with dark brown butterflies printed around the hem her short hair kind of off-white, steel-rimmed glasses slipping down her small beak of a nose . . . hard bony body pale face and little teeth pointed and sharp like a cat no one but her mother could ever think of her as being pretty and besides weren't you in love at the time with your teacher Miss Murphy tall and slim with jet-black hair or with Nellie O'Dwyer or both of the above. But neither Miss Murphy nor Nellie with the bows in her hair and the spitting image of Barbie Doll was as accessible at that moment as skinny Maisie aged six in her yellow dress with the brown butterflies and her eyes closed against the bright sun . . .

21

Yeah accessible and at six and a half you were becoming curious about these things.

And so you bent over her quickly and kissed her . . . full on the lips . . . and the response you got! Quick as lightning she sank those little rat's teeth deep into your lower lip. God, it hurt like hell! –

– SERVED YOU RIGHT –

– Lucky you had enough presence of mind not to draw attention by howling with the pain and enough self-control not to bash her stupid face in . . . boy, you got out of there fast didn't you with the rich red six-and-a-half year old blood dribbling down your chin and onto your school sweater grey with a red shield over the heart.

You told your mother one of the laners from Irishtown hit you with a stone but that didn't save you from six of the best on your left buttock with the long hairbrush for getting blood all over your clothes . . . and that wasn't the worst of it all your pals making stupid wisecracks . . . like 'Was it courtin' the cat you were?' That came from Moonface Kelly and you went and hammered the shit out of him . . . and to add insult to injury the bloody wound became septic and left you with a deformed lip for nearly two months –

The whole incident had left an indelible mark on his subconscious which no doubt accounted for his nervousness around girls and may well have been why he remained more or less a virgin until he married.

– Yeah, she probably still gets a good laugh out of it –

Whenever someone opened the front gate it gave forth a high-pitched, two-note squeal: F sharp and C according to Collins and he should know. He would have lubricated the cacophony away long ago but Lucy insisted that it was her early warning system for impending callers.

She heard it now, singing its welcome to her lord and master. Semi-automatically, she patted her blonde hair, cut short, naturally wavy. She adjusted the floral apron over her

22

slightly protruding but most becoming pregnancy and opened the front door, smiling a bright welcome.

– God, isn't she lovely –

He took her in his arms and kissed her, first closing the door so as not to scandalise the neighbours.

From the pressure of his arms or the firmness of his kiss or some signal picked up by her neurological antenna, Lucy knew instantly that he had some important news to relate or to withhold. About the job in Dublin for sure!

Collins's antenna was equally sensitive.

– Shit. She suspects already –

'Love you,' he whispered in her ear.

'Me too.' She untangled herself as her antenna began to pick up other more physical signals that she had no wish to encourage in her present condition. He followed her along the narrow hallway admiring and desiring her tall, well-shaped body and knowing full well that the desiring bit was in vain. She had already served due notice that her three-month-old pregnancy was not to be trifled with. Not after all those years of waiting.

– Oh God, how are you going to hold out for another six months? –

– GET THEE BEHIND ME, SATAN! –

'I have a nice bit of sirloin for the dinner,' she announced as she went through the ritual of relieving him of his briefcase and helping him remove his jacket. 'Ready in twenty minutes.'

She took his slippers from the press under the stairs and handed them to him. Then she gave him another quick kiss and retreated to her kitchen. He stowed his jacket and tie, as he had been trained to do, in the same press.

– Ah how could she know –

He went up the narrow stairs, two at a time, to the large bathroom with the oversized enamelled bath, indelibly green-stained below the taps. The gleaming copper hot water cylinder beside the bath sounded, as usual, as if it had a

23

serious intestinal disorder. First, he dealt with his most urgent and important priority, aiming carefully to one side of the bowl so that the indelicate sound of water meeting water would not carry to the kitchen below. Then, fastidiously, he washed his face and hands.

– *There was a time when you weren't so fastidious took a bath once maybe twice a week changed your shirt and underclothes when the mood struck you put on whatever trousers and jacket you took off the night before unless you happened to notice a stain or two . . . but marriage changed all that . . . for the better . . . mostly for the better anyway . . . maybe your machismo suffered a bit when she started to decide the clothes you should buy but it worked out fine once you got used to it –*

Lucy had indeed modified his behaviour in many more ways than he was even aware of. But all for the better, of course. From Lucy's point of view at least. He could hear herself humming innocently below in the kitchen.

– *Too innocently. She suspects all right! –*

As he came downstairs, the smell of the steak and accompanying onions and new potatoes reminded him that he had been so engrossed in his search for Harry and Foley that he had skipped lunch.

– *Just try to keep out of harm's way for a while –*

He turned into the sitting-room, small with heavily patterned wallpaper that made it seem even smaller. Much too small for the heavy three-piece suite and the venerable walnut-veneered piano in the alcove beside the fireplace.

It was a fine old house, left to him by his grandmother and full of warm memories, but there was no denying the fact that it badly needed a major overhaul, a fact which Lucy pointed out with increasing emphasis on almost a daily basis. And now, with the baby on the way.

He opened the piano and gently touched a few keys.

– *All the lessons Grandma gave you on this and wasn't she the one that found out you had perfect pitch –*

'Play some Chopin,' Lucy called from the kitchen.

'Ah, Chopin is too romantic.'

'And what's wrong with being romantic?'

– Remind her of that tonight –

– ONE-TRACK MIND –

He sat on the padded piano stool, carefully, because its seat was dangerously off-centre from the bulk of sheet music stuffed into the box underneath.

He played a Chopin nocturne. Beautifully. His large hands were sensitive and delicate as they fondled ivory discoloured with age and use. Even though he didn't practise as much as he used to, his touch was really excellent. Lucy waited until he had finished the piece before she summoned him to the table and, as he wriggled his bulk into the dining-nook by the kitchen window, the letter in his hip pocket rustled again.

'Well,' she asked in accordance with the daily ritual, 'anything strange at the plant today?'

Of its own volition, Collins's right hand reached for his hip pocket.

– Oh Jesus don't –

He held the letter out to her. The business-size envelope was folded across the middle, slightly creased, warm and curved from eight hours of close contact with his buttock.

'What is it?' she asked excitedly, even though she knew it was about the job in Dublin.

– Now you've done it, stupid! –

The letterhead was a bright red scroll, announcing that it came from the Leading Edge Computer Corporation. It was dated three days previously, so she knew he hadn't been withholding the news, at least not for more than a day. At the bottom it was signed by Frederick L. Deutsch, who proclaimed himself Managing Director, Irish Subsidiary.

The letter itself addressed Collins with the familiarity born of a ninety-minute encounter.

Dear Brian,

I was most interested in our discussion with you on the 14th.

Your background and experience were indeed interesting and I was highly impressed by your obvious drive and enthusiasm.

I am happy to inform you that you are now on our shortlist for the position of Human Resources Director with our Irish operation.

Lucy gave an uncharacteristic giggle of delight and read on.

I shall be in touch with you within the next three to four weeks to arrange for you to visit with us again so that you can meet some of my colleagues and further explore our mutual interests.

Looking forward to our next meeting.

A strange thing about Lucy. Whenever she became really excited, she went completely deadpan. Now she was looking at him blankly. Her eyes, large, grey-green, usually lively and expressive, betrayed nothing of the emotions and calculations that were spinning through her head.

'Brian!' she said, slightly breathless. She squirmed her way around the curved corner seat and put her arms around his neck, cradling his head against her luscious bosom.

'I'm only on the short list,' he reminded her, his voice muffled in her cleft.

'You'll get the job,' she assured him confidently, 'I know you will.'

– God forbid –

The dinner was left to cool itself in a bed of congealing gravy. She kissed him enthusiastically as her mind savoured the prospect of moving back to Dublin. A four-bedroom house in Blackrock. Detached, of course; they could afford it, especially if they got a good price for this old house.

Close to her parents. A bright, well-designed kitchen where she could really work her culinary skills. The theatre. Meeting old friends. Entertaining. And, in due course, Trinity College for the baby.

In her slightly guilty heart she knew that Brian would not want to move away from Ballyderra, but men were not very practical about these things and she knew beyond any shadow of doubt that Dublin was the best place for both of them and for the baby. She'd find ways of making it up to him. And, in time, she was confident, he would come to agree that it had been the right decision.

'Mammy and Daddy will be absolutely thrilled,' she jumped up and went for the phone, dinner now fully forgotten.

– *Oh God now we're off* –

'You're jumping the gun, sweetheart,' Collins remonstrated.

In her excitement, Lucy dialled the wrong number and had to begin again. 'It'll be a great load off my mind to be near them, now that they're getting on in years.'

Her father could beat him in straight sets at tennis and her mother taught advanced aerobic classes.

– *Let that pass. Don't go inviting trouble* –

'Get the housing section of *The Irish Times*, sweetheart.' She was listening impatiently to the ringing tone. 'We'll see what's for sale in the Blackrock area.'

– *It's going to be a long, hard night* –

And for Collins it was.

THREE

The print on the wall, thirty-six inches by twenty, depicted an anaemic seascape dominated by a foreground of grey-green scutch grass. A barbed-wire fence hung limply between rough-cut stakes. Above the water, two bilious-looking seagulls seemed to be looking for a target on which to relieve themselves. Like all of the works of art that adorned the managerial offices, it was rented by the Company and could be exchanged in January, April, July or October. And at each quarter's end the task of searching the catalogue for something less nauseating duly found its way into either the 'urgent' or the 'important' folder, but somehow never into the 'urgent and important' one.

– Next time, for sure –

Three weeks had passed since the letter from Leading Edge Computers had arrived to disrupt Collins's domestic life.

But there was something else laying guilt on him too. He had not yet told Merv Andrews that he might be contemplating a job change.

– Correction. Lucy is doing the contemplating –

But it bothered him that he hadn't talked to his boss about it.

– WHERE'S ALL THAT INTEGRITY NOW? –

That struck a nerve. Integrity was a quality that he valued very highly.

The lunch-time hooter screamed in G sharp, D and B flat and he decided to adjourn the inner argument until he had some nourishment.

In the cafeteria, Collins fell into line behind King and Malone. An ill-matched combination, right enough. King, tall and skinny and absentminded-professorial looking, peccably dressed in faded blue sweater and jeans, shoes unpolished. Malone, short and square and darkly brooding, in his well-pressed dark grey suit, cream shirt, red tie. Platform shoes to offset his shortness of stature.

'Make way for the health and happiness man,' Malone greeted him, but it didn't come out all that sarcastic because Malone felt that, for a Personnel guy, Collins wasn't all that bad. People generally liked and trusted him and that was certainly unusual for people in his profession. His only problem was that he took his job too seriously for his own good.

'Holy God,' Collins complained, 'did either of you see Harry?'

'I think,' said King thoughtfully, 'that he's back in the stores looking for a grub screw.'

'Grub screw?' Collins knew little of matters mechanical.

'Sex at lunchtime,' King explained.

'An insulated screw, I hope,' said Malone.

'Well,' King sounded thoughtful, 'he had his rubber boots on.'

'What did he do now?' asked Malone.

'What do you think?' Collins shook his head sadly. 'Groping under the assembly line again.'

'Ah, sure,' King remarked tolerantly, 'a fellow has to keep his hand in.'

But Collins was too immersed in his own problems to appreciate the pun.

'Andy is having hysterics and his girls are threatening a walk-out.'

'Are you going to fire him?' Malone enquired.

Collins shook his head.

'This time he has to get a final written warning.'

'He'll ram it right up your ass,' Malone warned.

'I'll have his supervisor present.'

'Foley?' King said sadly. 'Harry'll ram *him* up your ass too.'

They arrived at the serving counter, where they were confronted by a small and very fat man busily and inaccurately ladling soup into little white bowls.

'What is it today, Captain?' Malone enquired.

'Pea soup,' the fat man informed him.

'Human or animal?' King enquired.

Captain made no response. Over the years he had developed a firm policy never to exchange unpleasantries with the paying customers but rather to pass scurrilous remarks about them behind their backs. He now bent his little mind to composing something appropriate to say about King and his antecedents at the first safe opportunity.

They accepted a bowl each and moved along to where Captain's wife, Aggie, a tall human rectangle topped with untidy black-grey hair, was dealing from a stacked deck of sandwiches. Captain, a leading local entrepreneur, operated the cafeteria service among other shady deals while he, in turn, was operated by Aggie, a fact which he had never come to realise.

Armed with their calories, they meandered among the rows of grey, formica-topped tables until they found the most favourable girl-watching vantage. But before the first morsel of food passed their lips a trio of quite shapely and irate girls hove to before them.

'Mr Collins,' declared the most prominent one, not wasting time on preliminaries, 'you'll have to do something.'

– *More bloody trouble* –

'What's the problem, Peggy?' Collins asked with an uneasy cordiality.

' 'Tis that dirty oul' hoor's ghost,' she exclaimed.

– *Oh, God. Not again* –

'Horny Harry rides again!' cried King.

'Not Harry!' Peggy snapped, ' 'Tis Captain I'm talking about.'

Her bright yellow sweater heaved delightfully under the stress of her indignation.

'God!' exclaimed Malone, 'the place is crawling with dirty old men.'

'True for you, faith,' Peggy agreed.

'What did he do to you?' Collins asked, fearing the worst.

'Didn't you see the dirt of his hands?' asked the girl in high dudgeon, 'and him serving food. Do you want us all to get gangrene?'

'Oh, Captain,' said Collins, 'Captain. Right you are, Peggy, I'll look into the matter.'

'That's what you said the last time we complained.'

'I'll have a serious talk with him. I promise you.'

Peggy shook her head emphatically and her companions followed suit. Three heads, one dark, one fair and one in between, rotating in synchronised disapproval.

'No,' Peggy exclaimed, ''twill take more than talking this time,' and the heads of her two sidekicks changed direction to nod their vehement support.

'Because,' Peggy went on, 'we're going to boycott the canteen.'

– *Jesus Mary and* –

In times of severe stress, Collins's power of speech tended to desert him.

'We're giving you till next Monday,' Peggy went on inexorably. 'If that oul' hoor isn't out of here by then, you'll have a boycott on your hands.'

'And shift his missus along with him,' chimed in the girl on the right, taller, but not quite as well stacked as Peggy.

'Oh, there's a pair of them in it,' added the one on the left, not to be outdone.

'And that,' concluded Peggy, 'is our last word.'

And away with the three of them, hips oscillating among the formica-topped tables, well satisfied that they had done their duty and been minutely inspected by the two most eligible bachelors in the company.

– *Holy shit* –

'Holy God.' Collins's voice announced its return.

Malone turned to Collins.

'Tell us,' he asked, 'how will you go about getting rid of Captain?'

Collins was already pondering this question.

'No trouble to him,' King said. 'All it takes is a certain thickness of skin grown only on personnel experts.'

But Collins would not be drawn in defence of his profession. Long ago, he had come to accept personnel-baiting as one of the universally accepted blood sports. In the Orient, employees are permitted to vent their frustrations by beating the hell out of effigies of their bosses. In the less civilized West, they provide Personnel Departments to take the beatings.

'Excuse me, fellows,' Collins said abruptly and went in search of his leader.

Mervyn P. Andrews hailed from Tucson, Arizona, and bore up well beneath the title of Director of Human Resources and Community Relations. He was a most courteous and pleasant gentleman who smiled permanently and made decisions rarely.

His importance in the organisation was highlighted by his three-window office, oversized desk, wall-to-wall blue carpet and confessional corner. The rent-a-masterpiece print on the wall was larger and more expensive than the one inflicted on Collins. It was composed of row after row of little dots, very black ones across the top and becoming progressively lighter in each row until they were a light grey at the bottom.

Confessional corner. That was what the less reverent lower orders called it. But its purpose was clearly spelled out in Company Office Standard Number 6A:

OFFICE STANDARD #6A: EXECUTIVE OFFICES

In addition to office furniture and fittings laid down in Office Standard #6, all executive offices (three windows or more) shall be furnished with three easy chairs and one polished coffee table measuring not more than 3 feet by 2 feet or equivalent area in circular or oval design. These items of furniture will be set out in an informal manner at a distance from the executive's desk.

Behavioral scientists advise that discussions with employees (especially discussions of a sensitive nature) are more productive when held in such informal ambience. It ensures that employees feel less defensive and more at ease than when seated formally across the desk from the executive.

Incumbents of executive positions (Director level and above) are strongly urged to make full use of these facilities.

In the rare moments when he was honest with himself, Andrews had to admit to some reservations about using this set-up. He had a sneaking feeling that members of the lower orders felt as ill-at-ease as he did when manoeuvred into such an artificial situation. But the shrinks said otherwise and, at the rates they charged, they had to be right.

As Collins came striding in, Andrews immediately sensed his subordinate's unease and added a reassuring dimension to his smile.

'Merv,' Collins announced, 'we've got a problem.'

Andrews knew only too well the true import of such a greeting. Unfailingly, it meant that said problem was about to be dropped right in his lap.

'OK. OK. Why don't you take a seat.' He pointed to the chair facing him across the desk. Confessional corner was not for his subordinates, who had to be kept firmly in their place.

Collins sat and peered at his boss between the two large photographs, framed in gold, on the desk top. The one on the right was fairly new, a head and bust photograph of his most recent wife. The photograph on the left was of his two sons by a previous wife or two, their bodies grotesquely encased in American Football gear, each smiling widely to display a gleaming expanse of costly and repulsive dental braces.

Collins reported in detail on the threatened boycott and Andrews waited almost patiently until the tale was unfolded. Then he picked up his telephone and dialled the Lakeside Hotel just down the road.

'Terry,' he said to the phone, 'I believe the last time we talked you expressed an interest in taking over our catering contract.'

Collins couldn't hear the flip side of the conversation, but the expression on Andrews's smile told him that Terry was indeed interested.

'How soon could you start?' Andrews asked, and he listened for several minutes to the steady flow of assurances of prompt, first-class service and eternal gratitude.

'Tell you what,' Andrews managed to get a word in, 'I'll have Brian Collins contact you to tidy up the details. OK? We must get together for a round of golf one of these days.'

Andrews looked smug as he hung up the telephone.

'Problem solved, Brian,' he said.

Collins rose to go.

'Just make sure you finalise things with Terry,' Andrews cautioned, 'before you get rid of Captain.'

Collins was quick to realise who had been elected to undertake the unpleasant and dangerous task of disposing

34

of Captain. He took his punishment like a man by hitting his boss with yet another problem.

– TELL HIM NOW! –

– *Shit no* –

Collins sat down again.

'Merv,' he said, 'I have something to get off my chest.'

Again, some of Collins's unease transmitted itself to Andrews but he held on grimly to his smile.

'Shoot,' he said encouragingly.

'Well, it's like this. I got a call from a headhunter a couple of weeks ago.'

Andrews felt that the new topic might be one for the confession corner, but it was too late now to suggest a change of venue.

Collins filled his boss in on the details of his interview and the letter that had followed, and Andrews found it increasingly difficult to keep his smile from dropping off.

'Leading Edge Computers?' Andrews asked when Collins paused.

Collins nodded.

'I know them,' Andrews told him. 'A chicken-shit outfit. Their annual revenue is less than a quarter of ours. I wouldn't do anything hasty about this, if I were you.'

'I won't, Merv.'

– *Let them shove their bloody job* –

– TRY TELLING THAT TO LUCY –

– *I bloody well will* –

– THAT'LL BE THE DAY –

Andrews was still busily lying in his smiling teeth about the bright future that lay ahead for Collins with Worldwide Electronics, and went on to lie even more blatantly as he assured Collins that he would be the last person to stand in the way of anyone who wanted to advance his career elsewhere. By the time he was finished he had at least partially achieved his objective of sending the guy away feeling really guilty about the whole thing.

As Collins was leaving, Andrews laid a final word of advice on him.

'Just hang loose, Brian,' he said too casually. 'If they come back to you with a job offer, come and talk with me before you commit yourself.'

– *A hint?* –

'Sure, Merv.'

– *A counter-offer, maybe?* –

The only difference between the little voices in Andrews's and Collins's heads was the accent and the fact that Andrews's little voice often spoke aloud. Even their vocabularies were similar.

'Ho-o-o-wly shee-ut!' said Andrews's voice quite audibly as soon as Collins was out of the office.

Quickly, Andrews pulled out his folder of useful business cards and found one which read:

Leading Edge Computer Corporation, Inc.

Joshua L. Greene

Vice President, Human Resources.

Within minutes he had Mr Greene on the other end of a transatlantic telephone line.

'Hi, Josh', he announced, 'Merv Andrews here. Worldwide Electronics.'

'Hiya Merv,' Green responded enthusiastically, wondering what the hell this guy wanted from him.

They smalltalked for a while, mostly about the management seminar at which they had briefly met a year or so ago, and when that topic began to run dry, Andrews came to the point.

'Josh,' he said, 'I understand some people from your new subsidiary in Ireland have interviewed my back-up guy for their Personnel slot.'

Josh denied any knowledge of this and he might even

have been telling the truth.

Andrews went on, smiling-voiced, to point out that their respective companies would be competing for the same kind of people in Ireland, that the country was small and that it would be of little benefit to either organisation if they got into a pissing contest. Josh agreed wholeheartedly and Andrews proposed a tacit agreement that neither group would poach people from the other. Josh agreed again and ended up promising to persuade his colleagues to keep their hands off Worldwide Electronics employees.

They hung up with expressions of mutual trust and regard and Josh immediately got on the telephone to Frederick J. Deutsch.

'Fred,' Greene announced, 'I just had a call from the Director of Human Resources at Worldwide Electronics in Ireland.'

'Yeah?' Fred was a man of few words.

'He tells me you interviewed his number two guy.'

'Yeah. Guy by the name of Collins.'

'My friend would like you to keep your hands off.'

There was silence at Fred's end for a moment.

'That means,' Fred suggested, 'they wouldn't like to lose him.'

'Exactly.'

'And that means,' Fred went on, 'he could be just the fuckin' guy we need.'

'Exactly.'

FOUR

'There you are!' cried Collins triumphantly and Horny Harry realised that he was trapped.

Quickly, he pulled a ball-pane hammer from the pocket of his blue overalls and assumed an industrious pose at the workbench.

'How ya?' A grimace that might be misinterpreted as friendly showed through Harry's matted beard.

'I've been looking for you all day,' Collins complained.

'Ah, sure they do keep me on the go, like,' Harry responded, wondering how the hell's blazes Collins had ferreted him out in his favourite resting place behind the tool crib.

Collins looked at him more in sorrow than in anger.

'You've been at it again,' he said accusingly.

'At what now?'

'Messing under the line with the girls.'

'Who says?' Harry demanded.

'I had another deputation up from line three.'

'Is it them bloody biddies?' Harry roared, and Collins regretted that Harry's supervisor had such a talent for being somewhere else whenever trouble loomed. Harry, at six three, had a two-inch height advantage. On the other hand, Collins was younger and far fitter but the ball-pane hammer, tightly clutched in Harry's fist was also a significant factor in the equation.

'Comereta me,' Harry rummaged about in his whiskers to uncover a mottle of adhesive plasters.

'Looka what them shitehawks done to me! An' looka!' He held up his still-blistered hand for sympathy, 'What the new wan done to me hand.'

'That was two written warnings ago.'

'Sure wasn't I only checkin' out the electrics.'

'It seems,' Collins suggested, 'you got your wires crossed somewhere.'

'Ah,' Harry laughed contemptuously, 'who'd listen to them amadhauns anyway.'

'I had to listen to them,' Collins informed him, 'and I have a final written warning here for you.'

Harry realised that diversionary tactics were called for.

'Comereta me,' he challenged, 'what are ye going to do about the bus?'

'What bus?' Collins asked.

'The bloody Ardnaskeeha bus. It broke down this morning. Two hours late it was. With twenty-one of our girls on it.'

– Andy nearly wet his pants when they didn't show up –

'What about it?'

'The girls'll have to be paid for the two hours they're after losin'.'

'You must be joking!'

'It wasn't their feckin' fault they were late,' Harry argued.

'We can't pay people for work they didn't do.'

'Well if ye don't pay them,' said Harry, 'I'm going to bloody well slap a picket on the bloody place.'

– Jesus, Mary and Joseph –

– LANGUAGE! –

Collins forgot the presence of the ball-pane hammer.

'Who the hell do you think you are?' he demanded angrily.

'I'll tell you who I am.' Harry sounded smug now. 'I'm the actin' feckin' shop steward. That's who I am.'

Collins's jaw dropped emphatically and his mind went blank.

'Pakie D'Arcy is after going home sick,' Harry gloated, 'an' I'm standin' in for him as shop steward.'

– *I don't believe this* –

'I don't believe it!' said Collins, now entering the first phase of shock.

'Ring the feckin' Union office,' Harry suggested.

Forgotten was the little matter of the written warning.

'You can't picket the place!' Collins insisted.

'Who says?'

'The Union agreement clearly states: "No industrial action shall take place until and unless all steps of the grievance procedure have been fully applied."'

'Feck the Union agreement,' Harry cried out with passion. 'We'll fight for our rights.'

'What rights?'

'Any feckin' rights we like.'

Collins sensed that it was now his turn to adopt a change of tactics. He drew a deep breath.

'Now you listen to me . . . ' he shouted.

– BACK OFF! –

Collins took a moment to swallow some bile.

'You'd better think twice,' he warned with unconvincing force, 'before you do anything foolish.' And on that note he beat a quick and undignified retreat.

As soon as Harry had satisfied himself that there was no danger of a counter-attack, he locked the front of his overall belt in a convenient bench-vice. Then he leaned back and, supported at the middle by the belt, he went back to sleep for himself in an upright position.

Andrews sat at apparent ease in the organisation's most sumptuous confessional corner. The two-seater couch and matching easy chairs were ivory coloured and grouped around a low glass and brass table. Across the table from him, trim and elegant sat Jennifer J. Carey, owner of the confessional corner, Managing Director of Worldwide Electronics

40

(Ireland) Ltd and a woman to be reckoned with.

Andrews had given further serious thought to his conversation with his good friend Josh Green of Leading Edge. He had asked himself what he would have done in Josh's place and the answer had given him a distinctly uneasy feeling. What if Josh was so base as to encourage his Irish colleagues to indulge in a little people-poaching?

Andrews's three-year term in Ireland was almost up and he and his current wife were already making plans for their return to civilization, Pennsylvania style. The consequences of losing Collins at this point could be disastrous. The big boys at headquarters would never ship out a replacement unless there was a knowledgeable number-two guy in place to keep him out of trouble. If Collins left now, Andrews would surely be condemned to stay on until he had recruited and broken in a new backup. A year at least.

'Collins is a good employee, J. J.,' he told his leader. 'I'd hate to lose him at this time.'

'So what do you propose?'

'I think we might be able to justify a salary increase for him.'

'On what basis?' Miz Carey could be a woman of few words when dealing with people she didn't really respect.

'Added responsibilities. I could delegate responsibility for cafeteria supervision, employee health and safety, job descriptions and evaluations, policies and procedures.'

'Can he handle them?' J. J. asked.

Andrews, being highly skilled in the art of delegation, had passed these responsibilities down to Collins some time ago, without bothering to give due recognition or reward.

'With some help and guidance, yes.'

J. J. was aware that Collins had been doing those things all along, but this was not the time to put Andrews on the spot. That could come later.

'Sounds good,' she agreed. 'I think they'll buy it at Headquarters.'

'We could justify a six or seven percent pay increase,' Andrews suggested.

'OK.' J. J. stood up and smoothed the folds of her tailored grey skirt, signalling that the meeting was over. 'Fill out the form and I'll sign off on it.'

Back at his desk, comfortingly surrounded by his family photographs and the array of framed diplomas clustered on the wall behind him, Andrews went to work on a personnel change form for Collins. He pressed down hard on his gold-plated ballpoint to make sure the writing came clearly through all five carbon copies.

Normally these forms were typed, but this one was so confidential that he could not even trust it to his own secretary. Get it signed right away by J. J., ship it out by courier, make a few follow-up telephone calls and within ten days he'd have it back with all five approval signatures. Then put it into cold storage until or unless those un-scrupulous Leading Edge people made Collins an offer.

The telephone rang. It was Collins.

'Merv,' he enquired, 'you know the bus from Ardnaskeeha was two hours late this morning?'

Andrews hadn't known, but he did now.

'Yes,' he said truthfully, 'I know.'

'There were twenty-one of our operators on it,' Collins went on, 'and they're demanding payment for the two hours work that they missed.'

'They've got to be kidding,' Andrews laughed incredulously, 'they know our policy.'

'I thought I'd tell you,' Collins said, 'just in case.'

'It's the responsibility of the employee to get to work on time,' Andrews quoted forcefully, 'it's clearly stated in our policy manual.' And then the portent of Collins's last three words sank in.

'What do you mean?' he asked. 'Just in case.'

Andrews listened as Collins gave a blow-by-blow account of his latest skirmish with Harry.

'Hell!' said Andrews. 'He can't put a picket on us,' and his voice had almost lost its smile.

'I know he can't. But that doesn't mean he won't.'

'Has the idiot got no respect for the Union agreement?'

'Not very much,' admitted Collins.

'Look,' Andrews said urgently, 'get on to the Union office and tell them to straighten out that lunatic.'

'I'll try.' Collins didn't sound too hopeful, and Andrews hung up and immediately dialled the managing director.

'J. J.,' he announced, 'we've got a problem.'

J. J. listened attentively as Andrews told her of the strike threat and then, being a capable manager and well versed in the art of delegation she passed the buck right back.

'You're the expert in these matters, Merv,' she said confidently. 'I'm sure you'll find a solution.'

'But,' Andrews pleaded, 'do you have any suggestions?'

'Just one,' J. J. responded. 'Make sure you come up with the right solution.'

'You're a hell of a big help!' said Andrews, but not till after he had hung up.

As was customary in times of crisis, the Union official was unavailable and his whereabouts unknown, and Collins called Andrews again for further consultation.

'Keep calm, now,' said Andrews for both their benefits. 'What are the chances that they'll strike?'

'If the shop steward were here,' Collins replied, 'I wouldn't be too worried. But there's no telling what that hairy half-wit might start.'

'Have you got any suggestions?' Andrews asked, a trifle nastily.

'How would you feel about risking a lightning strike?'

43

Collins asked right back.

'Most unhappy.'

'Well, I'd say there's about a fifty-fifty chance if we don't pay them.' Collins speculated.

'Fifty-fifty?'

– *It's as good a number as any* –

'That's my best guess,' Collins said.

Andrews knew the exact decision-making technique to use in a fifty-fifty situation. From his pocket he took a coin and flipped it.

'O.K.', he said decisively, 'let's pay them and get it over with.'

'It could create a dangerous precedent,' Collins cautioned.

'So could a strike,' Andrews pointed out, and it was a point that Collins was quick to concede.

'Take care of it,' Andrews commanded. 'Dress it up as a generous gesture on the part of the Company, not to be regarded as a precedent, and all that. Get as much mileage as you can from it.'

Andrews hung up and, for a long time, he looked at the coin in his hand, fighting the strong urge to flip again for the best of three.

FIVE

It had been a hard day: the surreptitious 360-mile round trip to Dublin, the three-hour interview with Mr Deutsch and two of his henchmen and, hardest of all, the in-depth debriefing session with Lucy.

The Dublin interviews had gone well.

– Too bloody well –

Mr Deutsch had promised to get back to him within three weeks, but all the body language told him he was their first choice.

Beside him Lucy gave a little whimper in her sleep and he turned over and put an arm around her. She felt the comfort of the arm and snuggled back into his lap, then, even in her half-sleep, she realised that this could be a mistake. Quickly she put a few insulating inches of space between their bodies. His hand still rested gently on her protruding stomach and she wondered how long it would be before she had to stop it from moving sneakily upward or downward.

Minutes passed and the hand remained in place, just covering her navel. The lack of movement began to worry her. Something was amiss.

With a series of tantalisingly feminine wriggles she turned towards him and touched his face gently. He responded by pulling her close to him and she realised almost immediately that, in fact, everything was in perfect working order. He pulled her closer still and she was on the point of calling him to heel when she felt a wave of pity for the unfortunate man who couldn't really be blamed for the shortcomings of being male. Instead of chiding him, she drew her knees up to her middle, creating an effective barrier and forcing him to roll over on his other side. Lovingly and in greater safety, she put her arm around him from behind, so that her hand, in turn, rested over his navel. He waited in the hope that the hand would begin to slide gently downwards but he knew in his heart that his hopes were in vain.

– Think of something else –

– Killer . . . It was the Da gave you that nickname . . . a lot better than fatty-arse . . . the Da was two different men actually two different sets of memories . . . the tall wide merry man with the dancing blue eyes and the red face topped with fair curly hair and then after the stroke the wasted bitter-silent person with the thin white hair and the cloudy pale-grey eyes face and body gone all to one side in the wheelchair barely enough strength left in his hand to take the lemonade bottle from under the rug across his knees and sip from it through the side of his skewed mouth.

It was the big merry Da who was ordered to chastise you when Moonface Kelly's mother complained to the Ma about the hammering you gave her little darling so he marched you back into the old storeroom between the shop and the kitchen where he kept the three-foot ruler for measuring linoleum and administering corporal punishment as the occasion demanded and as soon as he had the door closed he takes you by the shoulders bends down until his dancing eyes are level with yours you could get the sharp-sweet smell off his breath tell me about it says he and you knew from his tone that there would be no punishment this time.

Your lip was just beginning to fester after Maisie Neligan's fangs very big for your age and very overweight Frank said you had the most kickable arse in the county which was probably true because the other kids used to take great delight in burying their boots in your backside fatty-arse they called you then and you never once let them see how you really felt then along comes Moonface Kelly and takes a look at your deformed lip and

46

says hey fatty-arse must have been courting the cat and it bit him and before you realised what you were doing you were charging at him with both arms flailing like windmills and the next thing you knew there was Moonface lying on his back his mouth hanging open like a torn pocket blood oozing from his nose and he screaming like a stuck pig reminded you of the first trout you ever landed up in Lochanoir and saw it floundering helplessly on the grassy turf. 'So now for you,' was all you could think of to say to Moonface and away you waddled.

Killer Collins said the Da as proud of you as he was the day you caught that brown trout your stomach turned when the da took the fish in his huge hands and twisted the head back to break its neck when he saw your face he explained that it was kinder to break its neck than to let it die slowly for the want of oxygen but after that you tried not to catch any more fish although you went with him as often as you could up to Lochanoir and Lough Ard and the Owenderra River upstream from the town the two bottles of lemonade he always brought along one for you and one for himself and it wasn't until much later that you learned it wasn't lemonade in his bottle and they had told him the whiskey would be the death of him which it was in the end but the big blue-eyed Da was proud of you that day in the store room and he called you killer and then told you to start yelling while he was slapping the ruler down on his own hardened palm six times altogether and you bawled as if he was killing you and the two of you nearly fell down with the laughing and the Ma giving out to him afterwards for being too hard on you I wonder was she really fooled by it must ask her sometime though listening to her reminiscing about those days you'd wonder if she remembers anything the way it really was. Or if you do for that matter –

Finally he fell asleep and dreamed about a brown trout chasing him along O'Connell Street, while Maisie Neligan, in a yellow dress with brown butterflies stood on the path bursting her sides laughing at him.

SIX

Paul K. Haley sat impatiently in his three-window office, cocooned in dense cigar smoke, waiting for his minions to show for the department meeting. Apart from Haley himself, the most striking feature of the office was the imitation teak desk which surrounded him on three sides. The main phalanx, positioned protectively between him and the door, was clear of all clutter except for the compulsory photograph of his current wife and three teenage boys and a gilt statuette of Atlas holding up the globe, won in a body-building contest many years earlier and many pounds lighter. The left wing of the desk sagged under an unruly pile of radio intestines and circuit boards. The right wing mushroomed out into a circular tabletop, around which he could hold meetings without having to leave the defensive bastion of his desk.

Haley himself was a giant of a man whose air of confidence and thirty-year pin impressed all who knew him not. In his earlier days he had somehow managed to acquire an engineering degree, but his most outstanding qualification was the special niche that he occupied in the Company's folklore. The mammoth Philadelphian was one of Worldwide Electronics's two longest serving employees, sharing that distinction with one Philip de Briggi, who now happened to be the Corporation's President and Chief Executive. It was a qualification that commanded the highest esteem from Haley's long succession of superiors. Especially as each one, in turn, came to the realisation that it was time for Haley to move on. All of their training and instincts warned them that the only politically safe way to dispose of the man while a few survivors still remained was to recommend him for promotion into somebody else's unsuspecting territory. But vast though the Company's resources were, they had their limits, and, with thirty-one years of unswerving loyalty and ineptitude beneath his belt, Haley had succeeded in plough- ing his furrow of disaster through just about every field of Company endeavour. They had finally run out of hiding- places for the man's natural talent for destruction. And then, in the organisation's greatest hour of need, someone conceived the idea of an Irish operation with generous grants and tax-free entrée to European markets and Haley was instantly given an obscure assignment to keep him out of harm's way until the new offspring could be nurtured to sufficient strength to withstand the shock. Then they created him Director of Engineering for Ireland and, with minimum ceremony and maximum dispatch, they turned him loose on the unsuspecting Emerald Isle.

Haley looked up irritably as his three subordinates eventually arrived. In single file they came with O'Keeffe, the design engineer, ostentatiously in the lead. He was the senior member of the group and driven by a constant need to demonstrate the fact, as much for his own benefit as for others. Though only thirty-one, his pale hair was already retreating from his pale forehead and he was beginning to suspect the onset of an ulcer. His most outstanding feature was his Adam's apple, prominent and wedge-shaped, with a tendency to bob furiously up and down like a yo-yo whenever he felt stressed, which was frequently.

Behind O'Keeffe came Malone, handsome, stocky, solidly built, with an intense look about him. Nattily dressed in double- breasted navy and walking as tall as his five foot six would allow. He was the methods engineer and probably performed some useful function which Haley had yet to identify.

Finally came the quality engineer, William Alphonsus King, built like a weed, stoop-shouldered, unsmiling, all knees and elbows. Attired in customary faded jeans and oversize sweater and wearing his normal, slightly lost expression behind wire-rimmed glasses.

Haley made a mental note to get someone to admonish King about his dress code.

King and Malone bowed formally from the waist as was their custom on entering his domain and Haley once more had the feeling, which he did not want confirmed, that he was in some way being given the treatment.

'You guys are late again,' he said accusingly.

'Sorry,' muttered O'Keeffe, jigging his Adam's apple athletically, 'I was trying to round these fellows up.'

'Are we late?' King sounded surprised.

'When will you Irish learn,' Haley demanded, 'that punctuality spells efficiency?'

'Your watch wouldn't be fast, by any chance?' King asked respectfully.

Haley gave an indignant snort which caused the windows to vibrate.

'My watch is always correct to the minute.' He looked at his overweight Rolex, waiting for the second hand to rise to the vertical. 'And now it's precisely eleven oh nine, Greenwich mean time.'

'Greenwich?' King repeated.

'I guess,' Haley made it sound as sarcastic as he dared, 'you've heard of Greenwich, England.'

'Ah, yes,' King nodded understandingly, 'that explains it.'

'Explains what?' Haley demanded.

'You're going by English time.'

Haley should have dropped the subject right there but he didn't know any better.

'Ireland is governed by Greenwich Time too,' he roared.

'Jesus, Mary and Holy Saint Joseph!' ejaculated King,

50

looking in shock at Malone, 'did you hear that?'

'Ireland,' declared Malone with pride, 'is an Independent Republic!'

'Remember 1916!' cried King, his voice charged with emotion or suppressed laughter.

Haley suddenly became wary. Before being unleashed on Ireland, he had been subjected to a four-hour educational programme about Ireland and its strange customs. He had carefully memorised the list of things to watch out for:

STEERING WHEEL ON WRONG SIDE OF CAR.

THEY DRIVE ON THE WRONG SIDE OF THE ROAD.

THEY TEND TO DRINK TOO MUCH.

THEY TEND TO BE ARGUMENTATIVE.

THEY DON'T SHOWER AS OFTEN AS AMERICANS AND MANY DO NOT USE DEODORANTS.

THEY ARE RARELY ON TIME FOR ANYTHING.

THEY ARE QUICK TO PROMISE BUT SLOW TO DELIVER.

THEY LOVE AMERICANS.

NEVER GET INTO DISCUSSIONS WITH THEM ON MATTERS OF RELIGION, SEX OR POLITICS.

It was this last item that now sprang to Haley's mind. The discussion seemed to be bordering on the political. He decided not to pursue the issue.

'OK. OK,' he bellowed, 'we're wasting time. Let's get the show on the road.'

O'Keeffe's Adam's apple shifted down a gear. In his palpitating heart he knew that some day King would stick his neck out too far and the chopper would come down, and it was his constant nightmare that his own innocent neck might happen to be within range at the time, and he with a wife and child to support.

Haley stubbed his oversize cigar out in an oversize ashtray. From the top drawer of his desk he produced an equally large replacement and proceeded to light it ceremoniously with an oversized, gold-plated lighter. Of the five American expatriates, he was the only one who smoked, but he had succeeded in disciplining the filthy habit by allowing himself no more than one cigar at a time.

With cigar in full spate Haley picked up King's report.

'Willie,' he asked, 'what the hell happened to our final inspection figures last month?'

'Why?' King asked in concern.

'Now, look here, son. I've been going through your monthly report.' Haley's response was challenging but non-committal because he had only the vaguest idea what the figures actually meant.

'Is there something wrong with it?' King asked, but Haley had spent too many years covering his ass to be caught that easily.

'You tell me.' he demanded.

'Well,' said King, contorting one skinny leg around the other, 'since Production introduced those on-line inspection stations, our final reject rate has dropped by twenty per cent.'

'That's right,' O'Keeffe chimed in, in case King might get the credit, 'we've got a significant improvement in quality.'

'Big deal,' Haley grunted, and O'Keeffe reversed expertly out of the conversation.

'It's a step in the right direction, though,' said King diffidently, and that remark brought Haley back on safe and familiar ground.

'Jeez!' he thundered, 'don't let them morons out in Production hear you saying a thing like that. You gotta stay on their backs all the time.'

King nodded acquiescence.

'Give them bastards an inch and they'll take a mile.'

'True for you,' King agreed.

'Never let up on them! Reject. Reject. Reject!'

'You bet,' said O'Keeffe, attempting a comeback.

'They might even do a bit better,' King added, 'as soon as they get the new production specialist broken in.'

'Who?' Haley asked.

'I think his name is Freely,' said King.

'That's right.' Malone emerged from his brooding silence. 'Ignatius Freely.'

'What's he supposed to do?' Haley wanted to know.

'What's any of them supposed to do?' King asked, and Haley thumped the desk approvingly, causing a small landslide among the radio components on his left flank.

'Too goddam right!' he shouted, his face turning purple with pleasure. 'Keep after the bastards. Never let up!'

'Gotcha!' agreed King.

'Another thing, Willie,' said Haley more gently, 'I got a problem with your objectives for the coming month.'

King looked concerned again.

'Too many objectives. Unrealistic!' Haley tossed the report across the desk.

'Do you think so?' King peered uncertainly at the report.

'When you're in the game as long as I am,' Haley told him tolerantly, 'you'll learn you gotta be realistic about objectives, son.'

King gave a nod of respectful assent.

'Take it away and pull out half of them,' Haley advised. 'Spread them out over the next two or three months.'

'Will do.'

'These objectives go to the MD, you know.' Haley sledgehammered his point home. 'We wouldn't want this department submitting objectives and then failing to meet them, would we?'

'Definitely not!'

'OK.' Haley turned his attention on O'Keeffe and his scowl returned.

'What the hell,' he enquired, 'is this problem with the printed circuit boards?'

53

O'Keeffe swallowed a lump of hard air, manoeuvering it with difficulty past his thoracic yo-yo.

'Some of the boards are tending to warp at the corners,' he said.

'Goddam it,' Haley was shouting again, 'your report tells me that. What I want to know is how many, at what stage, since when? And especially, why?'

'It began to appear last Monday,' O'Keeffe said. 'And the warping seems to develop just after they pass over the solder bath.'

'What the hell is causing it?' Haley insisted.

'I'm analysing that,' O'Keeffe told him. 'It says in my report . . . '

'The hell with your report,' Haley boomed, 'I want the cause.'

'Could it be the new supplier?' King asked meekly.

'What do you mean, the new supplier?' Haley snapped.

'Could the new supplier be sending us defective boards?'

'Willie,' Haley was less than tolerant, 'don't talk through your ass. They're top class suppliers.'

'Right!' agreed O'Keeffe, glad of the opportunity to divert Haley's anger in another direction, 'The suppliers were thoroughly evaluated before we bought any of their boards.'

'You bet your ass they were,' Haley roared, 'I evaluated them personally.'

'And besides,' O'Keeffe added, 'we've been getting shipments of the new boards for the past three months. And this warping problem is less than a week old.'

'Correct,' Haley concluded, 'so quit talking through your ass, OK?'

King bowed his head penitently and began to polish his glasses with the waistband of his sweater.

The telephone rang.

'Yeah?' Haley shouted at the mouthpiece. 'Yes, J. J.?' he amended politely when he realised who was at the other end.

'If you're not involved in anything very important,' the Managing Director asked with her customary courtesy, 'would you mind coming up to my office?' and Haley's heart crashdived for cover in his lower gut, as was its custom when summoned to the presence of a superior being. Not that it necessarily portended disaster, but there was always a fair chance that it might.

'Sure thing, J. J.,' he said cheerfully, 'be right there.' He turned to his little group. 'Sorry, guys,' he said, 'I got to go see the MD. We'll pick this up later, OK?'

Haley pulled on his jacket, large enough to make a small tent, blindingly patterned in a blue, green and yellow check that would be the envy of any television sportscaster.

As Haley turned to go, King and Malone bowed deeply once more, almost trapping him into reciprocity.

'You,' Haley beamed his scowl on O'Keeffe. 'Get that PCB thing resolved – fast. OK?' and off he marched briskly, still wearing his cigar, all the way up the long corridor, passing Thank You for Not Smoking signs at regular intervals and exuding strength and confidence for the benefit of all onlookers.

As soon as Haley was unsafely out of sight, King picked up his boss's telephone and dialled reception.

'Anita, love,' he said, 'I'm trying to get hold of old Freely again.'

'Isn't he ever at his desk?' Anita enquired testily.

'It's not really his fault,' King explained. 'They keep him on the move a lot.'

'I can't spend all my time calling him, you know.'

'I know, love,' King said soothingly, 'but if you'd just page him a couple of times and tell him to ring my extension.'

'Well,' Anita found his tone pathetically irresistible, 'just a couple of times. But that's all.'

'I'll remember you in my prayers tonight,' King

assured her. He hung up and looked at O'Keeffe, 'You didn't see him anywhere, did you?'

'Who?' O'Keeffe asked.

'The new guy. Ignatius Freely.'

'Ah you know him,' Malone said, 'tall, thin fellow, with longish fair hair and glasses.'

'With a Cork accent?' O'Keeffe asked tentatively.

'The very man,' said King. 'If you see him out on the floor, will you tell him to call me.'

'Right you are.'

As O'Keeffe went out to cast a doleful eye over the warping circuit boards, King passed his report to Malone.

'Do me a favour,' he asked, 'cross out half my objectives for me?'

'How the hell would I know which ones to cross out?' Malone demanded.

'Makes no difference,' King informed him, 'they're all accomplished anyway.'

'You're kidding!'

'What I get done one month becomes my next month's objectives.'

'Jesus!' Malone shook his head in wonder and admiration.

'Well,' King explained nasally, 'you gotta be realistic about objectives, son.'

SEVEN

Pakie D'Arcy came quietly into the office, which was enough to give Collins an uneasy feeling. Pakie, in his early thirties, was totally bald, small, sharp and thin and with a broad masochistic streak that made him a natural for shop-stewardship.

'Good morning, Brian,' said he gently.

– *Watch it! He only uses your Christian name when he's out for blood* –

'Hello, Pakie,' Collins greeted warmly, 'I'm glad to see you in the pink again.'

D'Arcy was convinced that the colour reference was a snide comment on his political leanings, but he decided to save that one up. 'Ah, sure I'm fine again,' he said, ' 'twas just a touch of the oul' flu, you know. But tell us,' he went on pleasantly, 'why did you go and stab me in the back while I was out?'

Collins was wise to the old trick of being knocked off balance. It had long been practiced on him by Union officials and Lucy.

'What are you talking about?' he enquired calmly.

'Didn't you make a deal,' D'Arcy accused, 'with that hairy bollix? Didn't you pay the Ardnaskeeha crowd for the two hours they were late?'

'They aren't complaining about it, are they?'

'No,' D'Arcy agreed, 'but everyone else is.'

'Why?' asked Collins, keeping a firm grip on his cool.

'Discrimination! That's why!'

Collins turned on a puzzled look.

57

'Bloody discrimination!' Pakie elaborated, 'against the people that came to work on time.'

'They were paid for working,' Collins pointed out.

'Right!' shouted D'Arcy triumphantly. 'And the Ardnaskeeha mob were paid for *not* working. Discrimination!'

Now Collins's cool began to slip away, unnoticed. 'You aren't suggesting that we should take the money back from them?'

The shop steward's shining dome waggled derisively. 'Come off it,' he suggested, 'we never give nothing back. You'll have to make it up to the rest of them.'

Collins began to laugh but even his own ears could detect the hollow ring to it.

'You expect us to pay people for two hours they didn't work?' he asked.

'Isn't that what you done for the Ardnaskeeha crowd!'

– *Oh sweet Jesus* –

– Taking the Holy Name again –

'Fair is fair,' Pakie insisted. 'Treat everyone the same. Everyone gets the extra two hours pay.'

'You have absolutely no justification.'

'Begod I'll give you justification,' D'Arcy assured him. 'If ye don't pay up, we'll bloody well slap a picket on ye. And how's that for justification?'

Collins reached quickly into his desk drawer and pulled out the pocket sized copy of the Union agreement, a slim volume tastefully bound in a blue cover with gilt lettering. He waved the book, fanning the air between their heated expressions.

'Now, wait a minute, Pakie,' he said earnestly, 'the procedure for handling grievances is clearly laid down in this agreement.'

'This isn't a grievance,' Pakie informed him, 'this is mass discrimination. And my members won't stand for it.' D'Arcy sprang to his feet and took two paces towards the door. Then he turned, 'And that's what you get for helping that hairy hoor to pull the rug from under me.'

'Why the hell did you make him your deputy in the first place?' Collins complained.

'My deputy?' D'Arcy laughed heartily, 'Suffering Jesus, do you think 'tis soft in the head I am?'

'He wasn't your deputy?' Collins asked weakly.

'Not if he was the only one left standing in the whole bloody joint!'

– Oh Holy Mother of God –

From the doorway, D'Arcy laid his final threat on Collins. 'Due notice,' he said, 'if the money isn't in the pay-packets next week, we're calling a stoppage.'

'That's impossible,' Collins argued, 'we're shutting down for the holidays next week.'

D'Arcy paused to think that one over. 'Right,' he said, 'the Friday after we come back from the holidays. No one can accuse us of being unreasonable.'

Then he was gone. As the full import of Pakie's message was beginning to sink in, the phone rang. It was Andrews.

'Merv,' Collins groaned, 'we've got a problem.'

'You mean the canteen boycott?' Andrews bawled. 'What the hell are you doing about it?'

– Jesus, Mary and Holy Saint Joseph! –

When Collins arrived, panting, at the canteen he found it abandoned except for Captain and his good lady. The corridor outside, however, was densely populated with loudly protesting employees and all Collins's instincts told him to take to the hills. But valour was the better part of discretion and he paused to enquire as to the nature and extent of the problem.

The buxom Peggy came busting to the fore, her yellow and black sweater ebbing and flowing with emotion.

'Didn't we warn you,' she cried, 'that we'd boycott the canteen if ye didn't get rid of the pair inside?'

'We're working on that,' Collins assured her.

'More of it!' remarked a plaintive voice.

'Ye're taking yere time about it,' Peggy remarked.

'As usual,' cried a supporter.

'These things take time,' Collins tried to explain.

'Oh, more of it,' said the plaintive voice again.

'His hands is filthy dirty,' someone else shouted and then, to compound the confusion, along came Andy Sexton squealing through the corridors and he calling on the Holy Family, whom he addressed like close friends, for an explanation of the tardiness of his crew.

Anita Merry's plaintively amplified voice on the nearby speaker contributed to the unholy din as she appealed to Ignatius Freely to telephone the Engineering Department.

'It'll all be sorted out,' Collins said as soothingly as he could manage while screaming above all the interference. 'Now why don't ye all calm down and go in and have a cup of tea for yourselves.'

'And catch gangrene?' exclaimed Peggy.

'For the love and honour of God,' pleaded a thin redhead, 'will you get rid of them before they poison the lot of us?'

'He will! He will,' Andy promised earnestly. 'Now come on back to the line.'

'When are you going to do it?' Peggy insisted.

'Look,' said Collins confidently, 'we're closing down for two weeks holidays on Friday week . . . '

'We know that, Mr Collins,' an impatient voice called from the crowd.

'And when you come back, the canteen will be under new management.'

'Ye're holding up the feckin' line,' Andy shrieked.

'Is that for definite?' Peggy asked Collins.

Collins's back was hard against the wall, and he knew it. 'Yes,' he said firmly.

'Fair enough,' said Peggy, who was quite tractable, except when excited. 'We'll call off the boycott – till after the holidays.'

'Good! Good!' cried Andy. 'Now come on, let ye.'

'We're entitled to our teabreak first,' Peggy pointed out and, followed by her supporters and Andy's mournful wailing, she marched into the canteen.

EIGHT

Back in the safety of his office, Collins telephoned the Lakeside Motel and made hasty arrangements for the takeover of the cafeteria service during the plant shut-down. Then he set about girding his loins for battle.

Wisely, he decided against holding the meeting with Captain in the canteen and so he summoned the little man to his office, where there were no sharp culinary implements to hand. In due course Captain arrived, also girded for battle and reinforced by Aggie.

There then followed a heated triangular discussion as Collins reviewed Captain's hygienic shortcomings and Captain, in turn, reviewed every dubious act of every member of the Collins clan for three generations back.

'And sure what would you expect,' Captain enquired of the world at large, 'from a bostoon whose mother's aunt nearly married a Black and Tan?'

Suddenly Aggie's fingers took a vice-like grip on her master's arm, cutting short both his vituperation and his circulation.

'Come on, Captain,' she suggested, 'there's no use arguing with this loodramaun.'

But Captain was not to be denied his pleasure.

'You little pismire,' he said, totally disregarding the fact that, even seated at his desk, Collins towered over him, 'I remember when you were running around the streets of Ballyderra without an arse to your trousers.'

– So do I –

'Captain . . . ' The good lady's fingernails gouged deep into her spouse's arm. 'Will you not be wasting your breath!'

'This upstart,' Captain cried out in anger, 'has the almighty gall to think he can fire a man like me.'

'We're not firing you,' Collins pointed out for the record. 'You aren't employees. You're outside contractors.'

'It's the same bloody thing,' Captain argued.

'No, it isn't', Aggie told him. ''Tis breach of contract. And wouldn't that be a matter for our solicitor?'

Captain had just drawn breath to let loose a further flood of diatribe, when the full import of his wife's words struck home.

'Breach of contract!' he ejaculated.

'Wouldn't you say that's what it is?' Aggie enquired.

'True for you, bejawsus.' His flab quivered with excitement. 'Compensation, bejawsus!' He trotted heavily to the door. 'Come on, woman,' he called impatiently, 'we're going straight to our solicitor.'

'Whatever you say, Captain,' said Aggie submissively and, without so much as a friendly word of farewell, away they went.

– CAN'T YOU DO ANYTHING RIGHT? –

– *Jesus* –

Collins sighed heavily and checked the time. Almost five o'clock and, though he'd taken enough punishment for one day, it was now time to go home to Lucy. She would be attractively busy in the kitchen with her apron tied askew about her pregnancy and eager to unleash her day's accumulation of pent-up words on him. But that was all right because she was beautiful and he loved her.

– *But she'll have to start listening to* your *side of the story no more of this shit about moving to Dublin* –

– YOU HAVEN'T THE GUTS –

He finished packing his briefcase and just as he was locking his desk he remembered that it was Thursday.

– *The bloody training session!* –

At five-fifteen the select group of trainees assembled in the training room, loudly bemoaning the tribulations of the day just ended. They settled themselves into positions of varying lack of interest around the large conference table: Malone, King, O'Keeffe, Phil Ashe and a few others not really worth remembering.

Collins shepherded the new buyer, Stevens, to one of the stackable steel chairs at the table.

'It's the two-year Company management training programme and it covers a whole range of subjects,' Collins told him. 'Management by Objectives, Performance Appraisal, Decision Making, Human Relations, Company Policies and Procedures, Finance, Marketing, Sales, Manufacturing.'

'Sounds interesting,' the new man said politely if not enthusiastically.

Collins cast a critical eye around the room to make sure that all the training equipment and visual aids were in their proper places.

'Right now we're into a three-week module,' he went on, 'on Effective Sales Presentations.'

'What's on the menu for tonight?' Malone enquired.

'Well, I'll tell you,' Collins announced. 'We've lined up a special guest speaker to give us a demonstration of an effective sales pitch.'

'Who?' O'Keeffe enquired.

'A Dale Carnegie man, actually.'

'How much does he cost?' asked Phil Ashe who, wouldn't you know, worked in accounts.

'Not a penny,' said Collins; then he made a slightly shamefaced admission. 'To tell the truth–'

– FOR A CHANGE –

'– he doesn't know it's just intended to be a demonstration.'

'What do you mean?' Malone asked

'This guy has been pestering me for months. Asking could he come and make a sales pitch to our staff.'

'You mean,' Malone asked, 'he thinks he's here to sell us

his programme?' and when Collins nodded, he added, 'You devious son of a bitch.'

Collins was pleased at the complimentary tone of the insult.

'Well, he's getting his chance,' he told them, 'and maybe he'll actually make a sale or two.'

King pondered for a moment, then looked around at the gathering.

'The situation has possibilities,' he said, with a faraway look that gave Collins a distinctly uneasy feeling.

Andrews came in accompanied by the Dale Carnegie man and friend. Of the three, the friend easily commanded most attention. She had long, fine, red hair, a remarkably skilful facial art-job and a slinky green dress containing a figure that instantly aroused every lech in the room.

Andrews led the Man to the head of the table for all to see. He was tall and slim and burnished to a brilliant shine all over, from his flat, glossy hair through his luminous polyester suit to his wet look shoes.

Andrews introduced him by name but, since none of the group had taken the Dale Carnegie course on remembering names and they were distracted by the friend anyway, the name passed them by unheeded and unregistered.

'He will outline for you,' Andrews went on, 'the advantages to be gained from the Dale Carnegie Programme, such as . . . ' his voice tapered off as he failed to recall the 'such as' es, and King broke into enthusiastic applause, closely followed by the others. The Man, looking mildly puzzled, acknowledged the applause with a slight bow.

Andrews deftly handed over control to Collins and slipped away to get in some serious work on his bunker shots.

'Good evening, gentlemen,' said the Man in a carefully mellowed voice. 'Before we get down to business, Miss Benson will distribute copies of our leaflet.'

Miss Benson did as directed, taking their all-embracing

64

eyeballs in her dainty stride. Then she moved to the back wall, out of their lustful view, and took no further active part in the proceedings.

'Now,' said the Man, 'so that we can get to know each other, I'm going to ask each of you to state his name.' He looked at King. 'Can we go around from left to right, please.'

'Ignatius Freely.' said King.

Most of the others gave their correct names.

'Thank you,' said the Man. 'And now if you will take a look at the leaflets, you will see that each one is divided into three sections.'

Dutifully, they scrutinised the documents.

'On the top portion,' the Man pointed out, 'we have listed four problems common to a great many people. You see those?' He got seven co-operative nods. 'Then the middle section summarises what the Dale Carnegie Institute can do for you to make you a better and more effective person. And,' he concluded, 'as you can see, the bottom section is a tear-off coupon.'

He paused for several seconds to allow any dum-dums in the audience to absorb all that information.

'Now,' said the Man, 'I'm going to ask you to study the top section carefully. I would like you to consider the four problems that are listed there and then mark an X opposite the one which you think is your own greatest problem.' He repeated it for any dum-dums who might also happen to be hard of hearing. 'Just mark the one which you think is your own greatest problem.'

They groped for pens while they studied the leaflet. The problems listed were:

- Difficulty in communicating with people
- Lack of self-confidence
- Poor memory for names
- Difficulty in mixing with people

Each difficulty had a box beside it to help them line up their Xs.

'And,' remarked the Man, very casually, 'as you have the pens in your hands, will you please write your names and addresses on the tear-off coupons and pass them to Miss Benson.'

The outburst of hearty laughter puzzled him, but there was no way he could have known that last week's session had dealt with the techniques of getting people on your mailing list.

'Next,' said the Man, when the laughter ended, 'I would like each of you in turn to stand up and speak for one minute about the particular problem you just marked. Remember,' he added reassuringly, 'there's nothing to be nervous about. We all know it's not easy to stand up and speak in front of a group of people. But we're all friends here, and I know you can do it.' His teeth sparkled in a blindingly reassuring smile. 'And,' he said, 'as a mark of encouragement, I would ask the group to applaud each speaker when he finishes.'

The Man turned towards King.

'Mr Freely,' he asked, 'will you speak first?'

'M-m-m-m-m-m-m-me?' King stammered nervously.

'There's absolutely nothing to worry about,' said the Man encouragingly.

King got to his feet and looked uneasily around. Then, in an earsplitting yell, he announced to all, 'I mu-mu-mu-mu-mu-mu-marked the fu-fu-fu-fu-fu-first one.'

'Yes?' prompted the Man, hiding his agony at the speaker's impediment. 'And why did you mark that one?'

'Bu-bu-bu-bu-bu-because,' said King, still yelling, 'I ha-ha-ha-ha-ve di-di-di-difu-cu-cu-culty in co-co-co-comm . . .'

'Communicating,' said the Man helpfully.

'With people,' King concluded.

The Man realised that to pass callously on to the next speaker could well destroy the poor bastard's confidence for ever.

66

'Why do you feel,' he asked, 'that you have difficulty communicating?'

'Bu-bu-bu-bu-bec-bec-' King struck himself a violent blow on the back of his head and the word plummeted out. 'Because,' he shouted triumphantly, 'so so so so-so-'

'Some?' suggested the Man.

'-times,' King continued, 'I ha-ha-ha-ha-hav-v-v-ve a bit of a fu-fu-fu-fu-fecking stammer.'

King sat abruptly down and his colleagues broke into polite applause, while the Man broke into a gentle sweat and hoped it was not going to be one of those days.

'Thank you very much, Mr Freely,' said he with a smile that was slightly gritted, 'very well done indeed.'

'And now, Mr O'Keeffe?' said the Man, ably demonstrating the Dale Carnegie name-remembering skill.

Tony O'Keeffe arose and performed a three-minute do-it-yourself analysis of his difficulty in mixing with people, and it was a relief to the Man to hear someone normal handing out the familiar load of crap.

Next came Phil Ashe from Accounts and he bemoaned his inability to remember names but pointed out that, in compensation, he never forgot a number. The Man felt himself slipping into the old familiar rut and was duly grateful.

Then came Malone. He got to his feet slowly, supporting himself with palms flat on the table. He cleared his throat and spoke rather hesitantly.

'I marked the first one,' he confessed.

'Why?' asked the Man.

'Because,' said Malone, 'I suffer from bleeding piles.'

The Man blinked several times in slow succession; then he cast a quick glance around the group but the faces were all serious and intent. He concluded that it must have been the speaker's faulty diction.

'Yes?' he prompted encouragingly.

'And,' Malone went on slowly, 'because of the bleeding

piles I'm very anaemic.'

The Man's faculties went temporarily out of service.

'And because I'm anaemic,' Malone went on with inexorable logic, 'I have absolutely no energy. And because I have no energy I couldn't manage to get past the first one.'

He sat down very carefully indeed.

After the applause had died down there was a lengthy silence. But the Dale Carnegie man had guts. He had gone down for a short count and he now came back up swinging. Though he remembered little of what followed, he went through his pitch by instinct and without missing a single comma or flash of the teeth.

When the meeting mercifully ended, and the students had departed, Miss Benson came and ministered to him. Then she began to sort through the collection of tear-off coupons. She read one, then a second and a third.

'Shit,' she said elegantly.

She went quickly through the remainder and was not at all impressed to learn that the attendance had included such personages as Philip de Briggi, the Corporation's president, her own revered leader, Dale Carnegie, and several person-alities of world wide repute from the arenas of sport, politics and other forms of debauchery.

In fact, out of the entire stupid bunch, there was only one genuine name to make the day pay.

'At least,' she remarked, 'he doesn't write with a stammer.'

The name was Ignatius P. Freely.

NINE

Jennifer J. Carey at age forty-one was held up as a shining example of the Company's commitment to equal opportunity, a claim which did the good woman a serious injustice because she had risen in the ranks as a result of her ability rather than her femality. In fact, if she had happened to be male, her talents would already have taken her to even higher levels. She was an attractive woman who tried, not too successfully, to hide her gender beneath severely tailored suits, all-concealing shirtblouses and frequent outbursts of strong male language. She was known to be a smart, competitive individual who had the knack of getting things done, and her assignment as Managing Director of the Irish plant was regarded as a testing ground for bigger and better things.

Each Tuesday morning at nine o'clock sharp Miz Carey convened her top echelon around her conference table to decide the Company's destiny for the next seven days. For some reason that could be plausibly explained by the Company's behavioural scientists, the decision-makers always sat in the same order about the table.

It was the Tuesday following return to work after the shut-down. On J. J.'s right, Director of Manufacturing, Myles K. O'Shee perched on the edge of his chair like a sparrow with bladder trouble. A plump, jittery little New Yorker who suffered from an obscure stomach ailment and an equally obscure Irish ancestry, both of which had so far defied diagnosis.

Next, going around clockwise, came the carelessly folded

frame of the Director of Finance, six foot of skin and bone, with the tattered remnants of a German accent and answering to the name of Fred Schmidt. No one had ever seen him enter or leave the plant and it was generally believed that he maintained a twenty-four-hour vigil over his precious ledgers lest some prying eye might discover what a magnificent accounting foul-up he had achieved during his two and a half years in Ireland.

Beside Schmidt rose the ponderous mass of Paul K. Haley and next to him, completing the magic circle, sat Mervyn Andrews and smile.

'My God!' J. J. wondered to herself, 'What did I ever do to deserve this bunch of wimps?'

Aloud, she said, 'Welcome back gentlemen. I hope you all had pleasant vacations,' and to spare herself any sordid details of where they had been and what they had done, she went on quickly.

'Gentlemen,' she told them, 'I've got two important announcements to make this morning.'

She paused for effect. Andrews obligingly injected a shot of anticipation into his smile, while O'Shee tried vainly to appease his stomach with a fistful of pills.

'Firstly,' said J. J., 'I'm happy to inform you that we've got the green light to start manufacturing the Model 660 radio.'

A murmur of satisfaction circled the table.

'As you know,' J. J. went on, 'the 660 project was Paul's brainchild. Most of the credit for the project belongs to him.'

Haley stuck out his thirty-year pin and cleared his throat with a modest purring sound.

'So I've asked Paul,' J. J. said, 'to put together a detailed presentation for our benefit.' She smiled at Haley. 'It's all yours, Paul,' she said.

Haley marched confidently to the flip chart at the head of the table. With a dramatic gesture, he peeled back the top sheet to expose one short, pungent message, printed large and in red.

THE MODEL 660 RADIO
OUR
GREATEST OPPORTUNITY

He gave them a full minute to absorb the caption's deep implications and then in a voice like thunder he launched into his homily.

'The Model 660,' he roared, 'is undeniably an outstanding opportunity and challenge for all of us.'

When nobody bothered to contradict him, he decided to go the whole hog.

'Probably the greatest in the entire history of our great organisation.' And before anyone could take him up on that one, he flipped the chart noisily over, and there before their very eyes, was a second stirring message.

OUR SUPPLIER
ORIENT ELECTRONICS
HONG KONG

'This outfit,' he told them, 'Orient Electronics, will do all the assembly work in Hong Kong. They will then ship the radios to us. All *we* have to do is install the mains transformers and stick our logo on the cabinets.'

'Will they sell?' asked Schmidt, always ready to start an argument.

'Sell?' asked Haley excitedly. 'You bet your ass they'll sell! We can undercut anything on the market! Just take a look at these costs!'

He flipped over to the next sheet.

'Get a load of that!' In his excitement, he threw a punch at the chart which almost put it down for the count. 'Look at those materials costs. Look at those labour costs.'

'How about quality?' asked O'Shee.

'See for yourself.' Haley produced a tiny radio from his pocket and held it jubilantly aloft. 'This one still has the

Orient Electronics logo on it, but we'll have our own green-and-gold logo on them when they go on the British market.'

He turned the radio on and, for its size, it gave out a surprisingly good sound. He passed it around the table. Each man fiddled inexpertly with it and was duly impressed.

'And there's another highly significant cost factor,' Haley added. 'By ordering a million units at a time we get an extra discount of twenty per cent. How about that!'

From there he proceeded to show them the proposed assembly layout for the two-twenty volt, sixty-cycle transformer line, production and inspection procedures, learning curves, standard times. His colleagues listened with ever increasing interest and surprise.

'Cheese,' Haley choked with emotion as he approached his climax, 'we can take a net profit of over one hundred per cent on these beauties and still leave the competition wondering what hit them.'

Redfaced with exertion and self-satisfaction, he collapsed into his chair.

J. J. was the first to recover from the onslaught.

'I think we can all agree,' she said, 'that Paul has done a very thorough job.' The others nodded in slightly benumbed accord.

'Myles,' J. J. asked, 'how soon could you go into production?'

'If Paul's figures are correct,' O'Shee's stomach was giving him hell, and he didn't care whose feelings he might hurt, 'and if Purchasing can get the kits here in time. And if Personnel can get me some competent people for a change,' he pulled a figure out of the air, 'my best estimate would be three months.'

'Not good enough,' J. J. told him.

'No way can it be done faster,' O'Shee insisted, confident that nobody had enough facts to prove him wrong.

'I want the first sets coming off the line by September

'five,' J. J. said firmly.

'Four weeks!' O'Shee remarked incredulously. 'No way.'

'Because,' J. J. continued, 'on September five, our President, Mr de Briggi, will fly in for celebrations to mark the production of the first Model 660 radio.'

'Oh,' said O'Shee.

They bowed their heads and pooled their brains about the table and, after considerable time and pains, they came up with a Plan.

Purchasing would get off their fat asses and order a million kits, express shipment, and thus qualify for the extra discount. Lines two and three would be converted immediately to make and install transformers and substitute logos on the Model 660, and forty-eight of their best operatives would be retrained for the job. At the same time, they would get busy installing further new assembly lines. A horde of new girls would be hired, trained and attached to the lines and a busy time would be had by all.

'Paul,' J. J. called as the meeting broke up, 'will you leave that radio with me, please.'

Haley handed the device over.

'I'll mothball it,' J. J. told him. 'In the highly unlikely event of a screw-up, I can always present this one to de Briggi.'

'Eighty new girls!' said Collins, and went directly into shock.

'Eighty-five,' Andrews corrected.

– *Holy Mother of God* –

'You can do it, Brian.' Andrews clapped his henchman on the back and wished he felt as confident as he felt he sounded.

'Merv,' Collins protested, 'it's all we can do to keep the numbers we have.' And he had a valid point.

Before deciding to grace Ballyderra with its presence,

73

the Company had done its homework. They had sent in a task force of experts to report on the viability of the area, especially in terms of the local labour pool. The experts had produced statistics on the number of local females at, or approaching, school-leaving age and had correlated these figures with the limited local employment opportunities. The results had been reassuring. But there was one vital factor that the planners had failed to take into account, and that was the local educational system.

Ballyderra's two convents could hold their own with the country's best in the matter of educating students to the point where their aspirations far exceeded their qualifications or abilities and, in consequence, factory work was considered a fate worse than death or unemployment. And so the erudite young ladies of the town elected to stay at home in dignified idleness or emigrated to England to find work in factories where the shame of it would not reflect on their families or their places of education.

This unexpected evaporation of the labour pool had forced the Company to spread its recruiting net beyond the bounds of the town and of reason, into the faraway hamlets and villages and hills of West Limerick and North Kerry, in frantic search of young ladies able and willing to feed the hungry assembly-lines. And in those remote areas, they were fortunate enough to discover the daughters of mountainy farmers and labourers and dole-dependants; girls of energy and dexterity who were not too haughty for such menial work, and whose parents suffered no loss of dignity when their daughters handed over their pay packets, sometimes unopened, each Friday.

True, with up to thirty miles of travel at each end of their eight-hour workday, they were left with little time or energy for normal social intercourse but on the other hand, the opportunities for other kinds of intercourse and similar mischief were proportionally limited; and besides, wasn't it a far better fate than emigration to heathen England.

'We'll pull out all the stops,' said Andrews trying to stir up some mutual enthusiasm. 'A major advertising campaign. Posters in all the shop windows. We could open another hostel. And, of course, our good friends the clergy will make the usual announcements from the altars.'

'But,' Collins pointed out, 'we've swept the country clean for thirty miles around.'

'We can go out another ten or fifteen.'

Collins shook his head and moved on to an equally distasteful subject.

'Did the staff meeting decide about the two hours' pay?' he asked, and when Andrews looked blank, he elaborated, 'The dispute over the late bus from Andnaskeeha.'

'Oh, that . . . ' said Andrews. 'We never got around to discussing it. We had more urgent matters to deal with.'

'We can't stall them any longer,' Collins said. 'They've threatened to strike if we don't pay them by Friday.'

'Hell,' Andrews smiled tolerantly, 'you don't really believe that.'

'It's possible, Merv.'

'But not probable.'

'I don't know,' Collins argued, 'there's a power struggle on between D'Arcy and Harry.'

'Well,' Andrews suggested, 'keep your ear to the ground and keep me informed of any developments.'

Collins moved slowly towards the door.

'I don't believe they'll do anything,' Andrews said hopefully.

'I hope you're right.'

Andrews could see that there was no room for hope or joy in Collins's soul and he searched for a cheery note on which to end the discussion.

'Oh, by the way,' he called, 'congratulations on the canteen change-over. It seems to be working out well.'

But Collins was not in the mood to take cheer.

'Wait,' he said, 'till Captain takes us to court for breach of contract.' And with heavy heart and feet he went back to his office, where he was immediately confronted by the apparition, unannounced, of Father Keenan.

The good priest was a large, bottom-heavy man, with gentle eyes and a gentle voice, always in a hurry and always unannounced.

'I won't keep you a minute, Brian,' said he urgently.

'Sit down, Father,' Collins invited rather pointlessly, as Father Keenan was already seated across the desk from him.

'I suppose,' said the priest, brushing some dandruff or snuff or something from his lapels, 'you're still taking on new girls.'

– *You could put that to music* –

'That's right,' Collins told him.

'Good. Good,' said the man of God. 'Because there's a young one from my parish that'd suit ye down to the ground.'

Collins got a pencil.

'Give me her name and address and I'll send her an application form.'

'I can do better than that,' Father Keenan volunteered. 'I can bring her in to see you.'

'Fine,' said Collins, 'I'll let you know when we're . . . ' but he was not allowed to finish.

'I have her abroad in the car right now,' Father Keenan informed him.

– *Not now for God's sake* –

But Father Keenan's stout efforts to stem the flow of emigration had made him the company's best recruiting agent, and with eighty – *eighty-five* – more vacancies coming up, his goodwill could well be vital. And anyway, the holy man was now standing by the window beckoning to someone outside. Collins felt that it would be both churlish and futile to raise further obstacles.

Collins pressed the button on his intercom and his secretary, tall, blonde and contoured like an exclamation mark, came gliding in.

'Liz,' Collins informed her, 'there's a girl just coming in for an interview . . . '

'Imelda Heffernan,' Father Keenan interjected.

'Will you give her an application form. I'll interview her as soon as she has it completed.'

Liz was not one given to unnecessary physical or vocal activity. She nodded her eyelashes and glided out again.

'Imelda comes of a very good family,' Father Keenan assured Collins, 'and she worked in a factory in Birmingham, so she has bags of experience.'

'Just what we need,' Collins told him.

'And she'd like to stay in the hostel.'

'There's no need for that,' Collins assured him. 'Sure we have a bus running from Ardnaskeeha.'

'I know. I know,' said Father Keenan, 'but she'd rather not be living at home. She likes her bit of independence, you know.'

Collins nodded understandingly.

In its wisdom, the Company had acquired an old mansion just beyond St Malachy's Villas and had converted it into a hostel for young ladies. For a nominal rent, deducted weekly from their pay-packets, the girls were provided with almost adequate accommodation. It was an arrangement ideal for those whose homes happened to be outside the range of the Company bus service or who, like Imelda, wished to be outside the range of parental eyes and thumbs.

'How long will it take you to interview her?' Father Keenan asked.

'Half an hour or thereabouts.'

'Good. Good. Good. I have to attend a Requiem Mass at St. John's. I'll be back in three-quarters of an hour to see how she got on.'

'Right you are, Father.'

'By the way,' the priest remarked from the doorway, 'I suppose you could start her right away.'

'Right away?'

'I left her bags out in the lobby,' he said, and was gone.

Collins sighed and went to the door of the office. The girl was sitting in the alcove across the corridor, bent low over an application form. She looked up at him quickly and his eyes gave an almost audible pop of appreciation. She was just about the loveliest girl he had ever seen, with thick, jet-black hair and a flawless golden complexion. Eyes that were deep, deep blue and very wistful. She was wearing a plain blue dress, tight, low and short, that did little to conceal its voluptuous contents.

When Father Keenan returned over three hours later, Imelda had been hired, inducted, installed in the training centre and looked over longingly by every male eye in the plant from Mervyn P. Andrews to Horny Harry and all the way back up again.

TEN

The Dive was dense with tobacco fumes and Thank-God-it's-Friday celebrants. In the economically seductive light from the single sixty watt bulb, one could just make out the pale glow of the heads of clients and their pints as they moved in ever-changing patterns, seeking out or avoiding each other.

Of Ballyderra's forty-four dens of inebriety, the Dive was by far the most decrepit and belonged to Captain, that self-same fat man who, until recently, had operated the Company cafeteria dirty-handed.

A very strange thing had happened to the Dive. Over the years, the town's forty-three alternative sources of comfort had been maintained in a reasonable state of repair. But Captain had been too mean and too lazy and had too many fingers in too many pies to devote either effort or funds to the upkeep of his premises. Large slabs of plaster had taken leave of the ceiling and walls, rough-edged flagstones heaved heart-sinkingly under foot, the paint was long gone from the woodwork and the windows had grown opaque with a compounding of grime and star-cracked glass. And so the establishment had earned the title of the Dive and a reputation that discouraged all but the least hygiene-conscious natives.

And then, out of the blue, along came that modern phenomenon, Atmosphere, and the Dive was the only public house in Ballyderra in a sufficiently well-preserved state of decomposition to possess that sought-after quality. The only thing needed to meet all the criteria was a substantial increase in prices and Captain was not the one to overlook such details.

And so it came to pass that, heedless of personal safety or hazard to health, the faithful flocked nightly to the place and Captain's accustomed evening solitude was rudely and continuously shattered by the impatient calls for sustenance, the drunken singing from the two snugs and the unaccustomed jingling of cash in the till.

Andrews was there, his ever-present smile lighting up the gloom and his ready hand clapping every back that came within reach.

Linked at the elbow to Andrews was his latest wife, Maria, tall, beautiful, elegantly sheathed in a long, blue jumpsuit, oval tanned face framed in artificial blonde, appealingly heavy around the bust and hips and viewing the world through limpid contact-lensed, calculating eyes.

Haley was there, celebrating his Model 660 triumph, and condescendingly acknowledging his Irish ancestry to all within loud hailing distance.

Collins came furtively in for a quick one before reporting home to Lucy. This, he knew, was living dangerously, but Friday had come and gone and the threatened strike over the Ardnaskeeha bus had not materialised and that called for a modest celebration.

Equipped with his half pint, he put himself into circulation, starting with King and Malone who were situated conveniently close to the bar counter and already equipped with matching pints.

'Saw your advert in today's paper,' Malone greeted. 'How many girls are you looking for?'

'Eighty-five,' Collins groaned.

'I doubt if you'll get too many women from around here to work night shift,' Malone told him.

The shift work idea was an act of desperation. He knew of some companies that operated 'granny shifts' from five to midnight and so he had run hasty advertisements in the *Limerick Leader* and the *Kerryman* promising good pay and pleasant conditions – *all the usual bullshit* – in the hope that he might attract some married women in need of extra cash.

– It's worth a try –

'Put Imelda on night shift,' King suggested, 'and we'll all volunteer.'

Andrews came smiling on his way for more sustenance and he managed to slap all three backs in passing.

'No strike,' he said to Collins with a touch of gloat. 'I told you.'

Collins nodded as his boss faded away into the darkness.

'I wonder,' Malone enquired, 'does he take it off when he goes to bed?'

'What?' asked Collins.

'The smile.'

'What smile?' asked King. 'That's a birthmark.'

There was a lull in the conversation as they lowered the liquid levels in their respective glasses.

'Whose turn is it?' Malone asked pointedly.

King sighed.

'What'll you have?' he asked Collins.

'Well,' Collins told him, 'another half-pint wouldn't do any harm.'

– What she won't know won't trouble her –

King went struggling towards the counter.

– Besides, she'll suspect you had more than one anyway –

'The wife is expecting, isn't she?' Malone enquired.

'How did you know?'

– God, is nothing sacred? –

'I happen to be observant,' said Malone, which was true. When it came to the feminine shape he was very observant indeed.

Peggy the protuberant passed by carrying a tray of drinks

almost as well loaded as herself. She paused to beam hazily at Collins.

'Sound man, yourself,' said she approvingly.

'How're you, Peggy?' Collins greeted.

'The new canteen crowd are really on the ball,' she told him.

'Thanks,' said Collins, savouring the rare moment of approbation.

''Tis a great relief,' Peggy swayed dangerously under her load, 'to be rid of that oul' tub of lard.' She began to move away, 'an' his oul' missus was every bit as bad.'

'When is she due to have the baby?' Malone asked, still on the subject of Lucy's condition.

'Just before Christmas,' Collins replied and turned to exchange greetings with his secretary, Liz, and to avoid further discussion about Lucy's pregnancy.

Peggy turned back quickly to Malone.

'Is it Captain's missus?' she asked in surprise.

'What?' Malone asked.

'Captain's missus? Is she havin' a baby?'

'Shhhh!' said Malone quickly, so that Collins could not overhear. 'They're trying to keep it a secret.'

'Why?' asked Peggy.

'At their age, you know,' Malone explained, 'people would be teasing them. Saying someone had it in for Captain and things like that.'

'I suppose you're right,' Peggy agreed.

'Don't tell anyone now,' cautioned Malone.

'To be sure, I won't,' she promised, and hurried back to her friends with the drinks and the hot news of Captain's afterthought.

Some time later, Collins, with three rapid pints inside him, and sadly out of practice at that level of drinking, became overcome with remorse at the thought of poor, pregnant Lucy at home, alone and dreaming up new tortures to inflict on him. He made hurriedly for the door, but he didn't quite make it. In the outer hallway, he found his passage barred by Peggy and several colleagues. They were well and truly cut and quite irate.

'What do you mean?' Peggy demanded, pointing an accusing forefront at him, 'by firing Captain and that poor wife of his out on the side of the road?'

'Wha-wha-wha-wha?' said Collins in reply.

'No consideration at all for the poor woman,' wailed one of the girls.

'And herself in the family way an' all,' Peggy added.

'Wha-wha-wha-wha?' Collins repeated.

'Oh, more of it!' said a familiar voice from the group. 'No feelings at all.'

'What are you on about?' Collins finally managed.

'I'll tell you what we're on about,' Peggy told him. 'We're boycotting the canteen.'

'Wha-wha-wha-wha?' said Collins, forced back into the old groove again.

'If Captain and his missus aren't back in the canteen by next week, we're boycotting,' Peggy repeated, and her backing group chimed in with a chorus of agreement.

'You hear that now,' Peggy concluded and withdrew her obstructions and was gone before Collins could retrieve his vocabulary. He went quickly in search of Andrews.

ELEVEN

When the sweet-spot of a golf club connects dead centre with a ball, the sensuous vibration that travels up the shaft and tingles the fingers is one of the most pleasurable sensations a man can experience in an upright position. On this sunny Saturday morning, Collins stood on the seventh tee without once having experienced this enviable feeling in the thirty-one shots he had already taken. Golf was one of the few things he did better than Frank, but not today.

– *Where the hell are you going to get eighty-five new girls?* –

He was last to tee up again and he glared down at the intimidating fairway. A par five, over a steep hump, then sharp right, up the steeper incline of the mountain itself. The fairway was squeezed tight between banks of furze, glowing bright yellow in the sunlight, thriving on their diet of lost balls and the regular spray of vituperation from frustrated golfers.

Under the critical eyes of his older brother Frank, and Bill Morgan, the local millionaire and friend of Frank's, he checked his stance, adjusted his grip, took a careful, controlled backswing, accelerated on the downswing. All according to the latest book he had read. The clubhead connected with a solid smack and the ball arced gracefully in the right direction, for once. Then, in mid-flight, the ball curved nastily to the left and the three men watched in silence as it hit the left side of the fairway and bounced merrily into the deep heather.

– *Fuck it* –

– LANGUAGE! –

Strong, shocked capitals.

'Oh-oh,' said Collins aloud.

'Oh-oh,' Bill Morgan repeated incredulously. 'All he says when he hits a shitty shot is "Oh-oh". What is he, a fuckin' saint or what?'

'Brian doesn't believe in using bad language,' Frank said.

'Bad language,' Collins said, 'is the refuge of the inarticulate.'

'Now he's calling me fuckin' inarticulate.' Morgan's voice rose in mock fury.

– *Morgan the stupidest idiot in the whole school failed the Intermediate Cert and got a job as a builder's clerk and wouldn't have got that only the builder was his uncle how could anyone so thick get so rich a building contractor now and bookie and coal merchant with a new Mercedes every year owns a couple of racehorses and a couple of politicians and not a brain in his head* –

They climbed laboriously down from the elevated tee and Collins veered away to the left to wade knee-deep in the heather on the off chance that he might find his ball.

Ballyderra golf course had been designed by Mother Nature in her most sadistic mood. In the no-man's-land where the fairly good soil of the foothills began to yield to the rocks, heather and grassy mounds of the mountain itself, a small group of fanatics had managed to clear a narrow strip of ground and declared it to be a golf course. On what was laughingly called the fairway, every lie was either up-hill or downhill, never level. But the greens were coming along nicely, except for the occasional rabbit burrow. It was only a nine-hole course but each hole was equipped with two tees, one uphill and one downhill, to give the illusion of a full eighteen holes.

Frank followed Collins into the rough to help find the ball.

'By the way,' Frank remarked, 'I don't think that advert of yours will do much good.'

'What's wrong with it?' Collins demanded.

'Oh the advert itself is fine . . . '

'So?'

'So who is your target audience? Who are you aiming the message at?'

Collins explained that he was hoping to attract older women, married women, who might welcome the chance of making extra money.

'Ah but where would those women be?' Frank asked.

'Around the town. And the outskirts.'

Frank shook his head.

'The people you're after are over there in St Malachy's,' Frank told him. 'The women in the better parts of town won't apply.'

Unfortunately, Frank found the lost ball and it took Collins three shots just to get back on the fairway.

Morgan yelled in delight as his third shot hit the green.

Frank hit his third and it stopped two feet from the pin.

'And fuck you too!' Morgan cried out.

'I wish that fellow would cut out the swearing,' Collins complained.

'Ah, we can't all be fucking saints,' Frank teased him. 'But the point I'm making is, how many people in St Malachy's ever read a newspaper?'

'So?' Collins asked impatiently. 'What would you suggest?' He picked a five iron and bent over the ball. Frank waited in silence until the ball was dispatched.

'I didn't want to say anything,' Frank remarked, 'but I thought you were using too much club there.'

He was right. The ball hit the green, then bounced away

into the hidden drain on the other side.

Frank won the hole with a birdie and they turned sharply uphill and left to the eighth, playing back in the direction of the clubhouse.

Between shots, and out of Morgan's hearing, Frank continued his job-marketing lecture along the eighth and ninth fairways.

Look,' he explained, 'the women in St Malachy's are my best customers. And whenever I'm putting on a special sale I print a flier and hire a couple of schoolkids to put it through every one of the 158 letterboxes in St Malachy's. That's how they get the message. The personal touch.'

'Ah, but you don't advertise jobs that way,' Collins argued. 'If I was in the hiring business that's how I'd do it.'

The ninth was a long par three and Collins hit his first good shot of the day, a five iron that actually hit the pin and settled down a few inches from the hole to an outburst of profane approbation from Morgan.

'There's a whole squad of women over there who'd jump at the chance of earning a few quid,' Frank said as they leaned backwards against the weight of their carts on the way down the steep incline towards the green. 'And evening work would suit them fine because their husbands – any of them who are working – would be home to look after the kids.'

Collins watched with some satisfaction as Frank's short chip rolled back off the green and settled comfortingly into the sand trap. 'Fuck it,' said Frank, smiling. 'But I'm telling you, a lot of those women would grab at that kind of job just to get out of the house.'

– *Worth thinking about* –

'Take it from one who knows, old son. That's where you'll get your granny shift.' Frank pointed downhill with his sand wedge towards the dense forest of television aerials.

St Malachy's Villas, named after Ballyderra's patron saint, lay sprawled and ugly between Irishtown and Knockderra.

87

A council housing estate built especially to rehouse the denizens of Ballyderra's poorest slums and to make way for two supermarkets, a parking lot and a cattle mart. A reservation of 158 three-bedroom boxes, soul-destroyingly identical and well on the way to becoming Ballyderra's new slums, the houses paddocked off into concrete-surfaced avenues named after heroes of 1916 and the Troubles, the street names printed white on green and in Irish only, a language strange to most of the residents.

– Frank knows all about St Malachy's all right –

Years ago, when the council had decided to build the estate, Frank had won the contract for supplying and installing electric cookers in all the houses. He was twenty at the time.

– And the Da was in the wheelchair and the business was going to hell bad times oh bad times the Ma sending you out to seven o'clock mass on Sundays and making you stay at the back of the church under the gallery in the hope that no one would notice the shabby clothes or the broken shoes . . . that council contract was our salvation it turned the business around all Frank's doing only for it you'd never have got to college you'd be stuck here in a dead end job working for someone like that bollix Morgan over there –

At the ninth, Collins decided to call it a day. 'I have a few things to do in the office,' he explained.

'Well,' Frank advised him, 'take my advice and send out a circular.'

'I'll think about it.'

Collins went into the makeshift clubhouse to change his shoes as Morgan went into a swearing frenzy over his drive off the tenth.

– MY GOD, DID YOU HEAR YOURSELF OUT THERE! –

– I know. I know –

– USING THE FOUR-LETTER WORD! –

–Only twice –

– YOU'RE ON THE DOWNHILL SLOPE, BOYO! –

88

TWELVE

Like the missing horseshoe nail that led to the loss of the kingdom in the old poem, events that pass quickly and seem of little consequence can sometimes turn on people and affect their whole lives. The following week, the second week of August, was lavishly strewn with horseshoe nails.

MONDAY

10.30 am Taking everything into consideration, including the prospect of litigation and the difficulty in clearing up the confusion about Aggie's expectancy, Andrews decides that it would be simpler and safer to reinstate Captain as canteen supremo and he orders Collins to make it happen. Collins complies, knowing full well that it is a no-win situation either way.

11.30 am Terry Moroney, hotelier and catering contractor elect, knowing which side his bread is buttered, bows out gracefully enough. His most lucrative trade comes from catering for Company functions and providing accommodation for foreign visitors to the plant so, in dignified silence, he pockets the cancellation fee of one thousand pounds offered by Andrews, without prejudice. At the same time he decides to raise his charges for accommodation by ten per cent for Company visitors.

1.00 pm To give Captain his due, though cruelly deprived of the opportunity to take the Company to the cleaners for breach of contract, he accepts his reinstatement with assurances that he bears ill-will to no one but Collins.

5.15 pm The first candidates for the granny shift show up. Collins's weekend advertisement had invited applicants to appear in person at 5 p.m. any evening and here is the first wave assembled in the lobby, all nine of them, average age forty, most of them with hair encased in amazing technicolour plastic curlers.

Dimpleknees and Collins's secretary, Liz, at time-and-a-half, have stayed late to screen the candidates and to pass the survivors on to Collins for interview. Dimpleknees pronounces two of the ladies to be myopic and incapable of seeing the circuit boards, let alone the tiny components that go onto them. Liz administers a dexterity test and fails two more for an overabundance of thumbs. Collins, harbouring a heavily sinking feeling, interviews the remainder and promptly hires all five, despite serious doubts about the mental capacity of two of them.

7.30 pm Collins drops in to see Frank at the shop and asks big brother to critique a recruiting leaflet which he plans to distribute among the denizens of St Malachy's Villas tomorrow. Frank offers some useful suggestions on ways of getting more sex appeal into the message.

TUESDAY
7.45 am On his way to the plant, Collins meets the postman who hands him another letter from Leading Edge. He reads it on the roadway, gives a grunt of disgust and jams it deep in his hip pocket.

10.00 am Martin Murphy, aged twelve and his ten-year-old brother, Brianeen assemble in Collins's office. Their mother, Kathleen, is a second cousin of Collins and not too well off. Collins issues his second cousins once removed with a hundred fliers each and instructs them to saturate St Malachy's Villas with them. He hands over ten pounds per man for their trouble, half to go to their mother and the remainder to be spent only when the job is completed.

11.00 am Frank Collins telephones an electrical distributor in Dublin and negotiates a special deal on a hundred microwave cookers to be delivered within twenty-four hours.

5.00 pm Four ladies of the same age group and general demeanour as those of the day before appear in the lobby. One has the signs of drink on her and is gently turned away. The other three are hired.

7.00 to 10.30 pm Lucy makes sterling efforts to hold her patience with her dejected and complaining husband and comes dangerously close to making a serious error in judgment. The conversation goes like this:

LUCY: Come on, sweetheart. Don't be so gloomy.
COLLINS: Eighty-five women by the end of this week.
            And all I've got so far is eight.
LUCY: Sure you'll be off to the new job any day now.
            – *Oh Jesus, we're on that tack agaiN* –
COLLINS: I haven't been *offered* the job yet.
[Lucy waves the letter he got that morning from Leading Edge. She has almost memorised it by now.]
LUCY: Mr Deutsch says here that you're definitely
            the leading candidate.
COLLINS: It still isn't a job offer.
LUCY: It is if you read between the lines.
COLLINS: [Shaking his head]
            He's taking too long to make up his mind.
LUCY: [Waving the letter in his face]
            He explained that. He has to go to America
            for some important strategy meetings, and
            doesn't he say plainly that he wants to meet
            you when he gets back. 'To – [she refers to
            the letter] – to bring matters to a mutually
            satisfactory conclusion.' He couldn't make
            it much plainer than that, could he?
[Collins sighs and shakes his head sadly. Lucy tries another approach]

LUCY: Sweetheart. Did I tell you about the lovely
             house Mammy and I looked at in Blackrock
             last weekend?
             – *She knows bloody well she didn't!* –
LUCY: Four bedrooms, two bathrooms and two
             big bright living rooms. Detached. And a
             lovely garden. And central heating.
             – *A recruiting bonus! Hey, why didn't you think
             of that before* –
LUCY: We could turn one of the bedrooms into a
             study for you. You've always wanted your
             own study.
             – *Some factories in Shannon offer bonuses to
             employees who bring in recruits* –
LUCY: The price is a bit on the high side.
             – *If we offered a recruiting bonus of fifty pounds
             for every* –
LUCY: But we could manage it if we could get a
             good price for –
             – *Oh, Christ, no!* –
             [Just in time, Lucy catches herself.]
             – *She's going to suggest we sell this house* –
LUCY: [Hastily]
             I mean – You know – If I got a good job. I
             could go back teaching. We could afford it
             with the two incomes.
             – *She was! She was going to suggest it!* –
COLLINS: For a moment there I thought you were
             going to suggest selling this house.
LUCY: Sweetheart. We could never part with this
             house. It means too much to you.
             – *Now she's trying to put you on the defensive* –
[Lucy touches his face with gentle, affectionate fingertips.]
LUCY: You know I'd never do anything to make
             you unhappy, sweetheart.
COLLINS: I know, sweetheart.

– See! You misjudged her again –

LUCY: You know I love you, sweetheart.

COLLINS: I love you too.

[They embrace. Collins buries his face in her soft, scented hair.]

– Eighty-five fucking new employees –

WEDNESDAY

A misleadingly normal-looking day.

9.30 am Collins discusses the idea of a recruitment bonus with Andrews and Andrews agrees to think about it.

10.00 am Collins starts calling the priests in the neighbouring parishes about local reaction to the recruiting notices they read out at the Sunday masses. The feedback is not very encouraging.

10.30 am The forms approving Brian Collins's pay increase arrive from Headquarters adorned with all five levels of hierarchical authorisation. Andrews locks the papers furtively away in his credenza.

1.30 pm The consignment of microwave cookers is delivered to Frank's shop.

2.20 pm Andrews seeks Jennifer Carey's views on the recruiting bonus, as if it was his own idea. J. J. approves in principle. Andrews informs J. J. of the approval of Collins's pay rise and they agree to keep the matter under wraps in the hope that Andrews's ultimatum to Leading Edge on the subject of pissing contests actually took effect.

THURSDAY

9.30 am Martin and Brianeen Murphy earn another ten pounds each distributing circulars throughout St Malachy's Villas. This particular missive has nothing to do with Collins's recruiting concerns – or has it?

WORKING WOMEN!!!!!!!!!!!!!!
BREAK AWAY FROM KITCHEN DRUDGERY!!!!!!!!!
HOW?????????????
WITH A MICROWAVE COOKER, OF COURSE!!!!!
QUICK, EASY AND ECONOMICAL!!!!!!!
MEALS COOKED IN MINUTES!!!!!!!!!
JUST PUT THE PREPARED MEAL IN THE MICROWAVE AND TAKE OFF FOR YOURSELF. WHEN HIMSELF ARRIVES HOME, ALL HE HAS TO DO IS SWITCH IT ON AND HIS WELL-COOKED DINNER IS READY IN MINUTES. SO GET YOUR TIME-SAVING MICROWAVE AT
FRANK COLLINS ELECTRICAL
TODAY!
AND SAVE POUNDS!!!
WE OFFER OUR USUAL EASY TERMS.
YOU CAN COUNT ON COLLINS!!!!

11.45 am Frank's two shop windows are transformed into an eye-catching display of microwave ovens, set against a lavish backdrop of pictures of mouthwatering microwave dinners and recipes.

4.45 pm Things begin to ease off at Frank's shop. In five hours he has sold and arranged hire-purchase terms for fifty-seven microwave cookers and has ordered a further fifty from the supplier.

5.15 pm Collins puts the finishing touches to a memo to all employees announcing a recruiting bonus of fifty pounds to each employee who brings in a new recruit. To discourage any dishonest practices, half of the bonus is to be paid when the new employee starts work. The balance to be paid if and when the individual is still in employment one month later.

He signs the memo, takes a quick glance out of the

window and promptly goes into a state of shock. From the front entrance, along the driveway and curving out onto the roadside is stretched a long queue of women. He counts them. Fifty-seven all told. He telephones Lucy to tell her he'll be late for dinner. She is most patient and understanding, as she has been ever since she almost made the tactical error of suggesting that they might sell the house.

Andrews, giggling with delight, is hovering around the mob of applicants taking Polaroid pictures with which to impress his superiors at headquarters.

7.45 pm Fifty of the new applicants are hired and instructed to report for work at 4.30 p.m. next Monday.

FRIDAY
4.45 pm Frank has sold another forty-nine microwave cookers.

5.15 pm Forty-nine applicants arrive at the plant and forty pass the interview. Knowing that some of the people he has already selected are not likely to make the grade in training, Collins wisely hires them all. One of the candidates shows him a copy of Frank's circular. It explains the sudden influx of ladies but raises the question of ethics. He is very angry indeed with his duplicitous brother.

    – Jesus, I'll murder him when I get hold of him –

THIRTEEN

It was a gentle August morning, mist blanketing the mountain tops, not a wind stirring the damp hedgerows, a couple of invisible skylarks tuning up as they rose haltingly towards the sky. The mists of the night had compressed the dust on the laneway and it whispered softly underfoot. As Collins walked along, his shoes left impressions paler than the wet surface and the smell of the disturbed dust caught his nostrils and throat. It was a good start to the day.

All was going suspiciously well at Worldwide Electronics too. The ninety-four members of the granny shift who had survived the rigours of the training centre were installed on the line and their learning curve, like the skylarks, was on the rise. The transformer assembly lines were up and running and the first million assembly kits from Hong Kong were neatly stacked in Stores, awaiting their transfiguration.

Now the only cloud on Collins's horizon was the impending return of Mr Deutsch from his strategy meetings in the States and the crunch that would undoubtedly follow their next meeting.

In fact, most of his mind's free time was given to this dilemma, either rehearsing the various scenarios involving Lucy or indulging in almost maudlin re-runs of old memories of the home that he might be forced to leave forever unless Lucy relented.

– Or unless you stand up for yourself –

– THAT'LL BE THE DAY! –

Below and to his left the morning mist had lifted off the town, though some delicate wisps still hung over the river and gently stroked the church spire. A few people, mostly women, were scurrying along O'Connell Street and Barrack Street. On their way to half-eight mass.

A shaft of pale sunlight pierced the mist and spotlighted the green patch between the school and the courthouse.

– *Didn't you practically wear a track down around that field when Frank appointed himself as your trainer . . . seven years of age and starting to learn the most important lesson of your life though you didn't realise it at the time that you could be as good as any of them even better if you tried harder than anyone else and so you trained and ran and all the fat dropped off and all of a sudden you were the fittest one of the whole lot no more Fatty-Arse but Killer Collins and Frank kept issuing challenges and you couldn't let him down even when you had to fight lads that were years older remember the book on boxing he got you out of the library . . . left foot forward left fist extended with elbow down so you can pull it back to protect your solar plexus right fist in front of your chin elbow down to protect your solar plexus as well with the fist cocked for a killer punch shuffle forward and back feet solid on the ground so that you couldn't be knocked off balance only whenever it came to a fight you just started whirling your arms like windmills and charged straight ahead and the enemy either ran away or was battered to the ground in seconds Frank always giving out to you for not following the book you're always leaving yourself wide open to an uppercut says he some of them managed to land a few blows before they went down but you never noticed the hurt until it was all over and didn't you always win thank God that phase didn't last very long because pretty soon nobody could be persuaded to come up against you . . . but it got you respect . . . nobody ever said you were brilliant but you tried harder than everyone else and it paid off . . . at*

97

He climbed through the gap in the fence and crossed the green lawn in front of the plant. A plaintive wail came billowing out from the plant and his gut told him that Horny Harry had struck again.

At his office door Andy greeted him stridently.

'My whole feckin' line is stopped!' he screeched.

Collins levered the little man into the office in a futile effort to muffle his howls.

'The hairy bloody hoor,' Andy yelled, 'he's after bollixing up my schedule again.'

'What did he do now?' Collins asked.

– As if you didn't know! –

'What do you *think* he done?' Andy began to dance energetically. 'He grabbed one of my girls by the you-know-what and she has a bump on the back of her head as big as a goose's egg.'

Collins pondered on the relationship between the point of attack and the point of injury, but Andy quickly put him straight.

'She pulled back when the fecker grabbed her,' he explained, 'and her chair toppled over and she banged her head on the floor.'

'Any danger of concussion?' Collins asked with concern.

'Feck the concussion,' Andy remarked, 'my whole feckin' line is down. I want that hoor fired this minute.'

'We can't do that!' Collins explained patiently. 'The next step has to be suspension pending an investigation.'

'Well suspend the hoor! Just get him out of here!'

'We'll look into it,' Collins assured him, anxious to buy a little time.

The phone rang. It was Andrews.

'What the hell is happening?' he shouted into Collins's ear.

'What do you mean, Merv?'

'One of the girls claims she was sexually assaulted,' Andrews bawled. 'Do you realise the whole unit has stopped work?'

'I'm just looking into it,' Collins assured him.

'Get that sex maniac off the premises,' Andrews suggested in a tone that brooked no argument. 'Then look into it!'

'Right!' said Collins decisively. 'That's just what I'm going to do.'

'I'd appreciate it,' said his boss sarcastically and hung up.

Collins looked Andy in the eye.

'Right you are,' he said firmly, 'I'm going to suspend Harry on the spot.'

'Sound man yourself,' said Andy approvingly, and off he trotted to tell his girls Harry had been fired, just in case suspension might not be enough to get them back to work.

Within twenty minutes, Harry was off the premises with a three-day suspension pending investigation of the incident and, to everyone's amazement, he went without a single blow being struck.

To avert any possible repercussions, Collins telephoned the Union office and, after the customary half dozen tries, he got through to Ned Barry, the branch secretary. Calmly he explained the situation, pointing out that the Company's action was fully justified and that the procedure laid down in the Union agreement had been followed to the letter.

The official could find nothing irregular about the Company's action but no self-respecting Union man would stoop to such an admission. Honour had to be upheld and a compromise, however small, had to be sought.

They were going through the usual skirmishing about immediate reinstatement without loss of pay, or at least a reduction of the suspension period, when Collins happened to look out of the window.

'Jesus, Mary and Joseph!' Collins yelled.

– SWEARING OUT LOUD. I TOLD YOU! –

– *Look at the son of a bitch* –

The son of a bitch in question was Horny Harry and there he was in a dignified one-man parade in front of the main entrance. Above his head he brandished a large, wooden sign. And on the sign was printed the clarion call to arms:

STRIKE! WORKERS UNTIE

The rousing words, misspelling and all, were printed in crude but large letters across a single narrow board which bore a striking resemblance to a crucifix.

'Get over here fast,' Collins roared into the phone.

'Why should I?' Ned Barry took umbrage at the tone of the request.

'The bloody screwball is after slapping a picket on us.'

'Who?'

'Who the hell do you think?' Collins cried out, 'Harry. Will you for the love and honour of God come over here and shift him.'

'I'll be over in two shakes,' the official promised and hung up. He then thought the matter over and concluded that the proper course of action was to become unavailable for a day or two and let nature take its course. Quickly, he took his phone off the hook.

Collins studied Harry's patrol pattern for a few more palpitations. He considered going out to try to reason with the stupid son of a bitch but, instead, called Andrews for a second opinion. Andrews called J. J. for a third opinion. By consensus, a wait-and-see attitude was adopted.

And so, through the long day, Harry maintained his solitary patrol and the first to face the daunting sight of the tall, hairy, one-man picket were the incoming members of the newly formed evening shift on their way to work.

There is something about passing a picket, even a one-man picket, that produces the same uneasy feeling as walking over someone's grave, but with one noteworthy difference. The man in the grave is less likely to come up behind you and beat you over the head with his sign. And when the sign itself is shaped like a cross, a further frightening dimension is added because a blow from such a

100

weapon could easily split a man from crown to crotch.

The would-be workers began to congeal in small, uncertain clusters. Some joked loudly to hide their unease, but most of them chickenly held their own counsel and awaited developments. However, not one among them was so base or so brave as to pass the dreaded symbol.

Shortly after five the day workers began to emerge. When they read the situation they hurried past with eyes averted and hoped that it would all have blown over by the following morning. They were the only ones to pass the picket on that fateful day and gradually the evening shift faded into the sunset.

Next morning the day shift returned, confident that the problem had gone away during the night but, to their dismay, there was Harry still looming steadfast and ominous between them and their livelihood.

The realisation began to dawn on them that they now had a problem. Their comrades of the night had lacked the guts to pass the picket and that left them with little option but to follow suit. There were, therefore, two courses of action open. One was to wait around in the hope that a passing truck might run the stupid bastard down, and the other was to come out stolidly in his support and force the Company to reinstate him and so get him the hell out of their path.

While the first alternative would have been the source of greater satisfaction to all but Harry, it could take an unduly long time to come to fruition and so a deputation was dispatched inside with the traditional one-out-all-out ultimatum.

Andrews responded with a lengthy message, carefully phrased so that nobody would really understand what he was saying, because he didn't know what the hell to say anyway. Under cover of the wordy smokescreen, Collins made further frantic attempts to contact the Union official only to be informed that the decent man had been called to Cork by the timely death of a relative.

But then, as the day wore on, a very strange thing

101

happened. In the morning, nothing would have warmed the cockles of the would-be workers' hearts more than the sight of Horny Harry being mashed to a red slurry beneath an articulated truck. Then gradually, almost imperceptibly, their collective resentment transferred itself from Harry to the Company because, after all, sure these multinationals didn't give a tinker's shite about the poor worker and anyway things like this were always the fault of bad management.

And so, by the time the evening shift arrived, the day workers were solidly and vociferously behind Harry and, uttering loud cries of support, they departed for home, leaving the matter confidently in the hands of their comrades of the twilight.

But the temper of the evening shift had also undergone a significant change. Twenty-four hours earlier, they had given Harry their unanimous, if reluctant, support. Now, in the harsh light of day and of reason, they had come to realise that they had already blown one fifth of a week's pay, and they were not kindly disposed towards upping the ante.

Safely out of Harry's earshot, a brief but earnest conference was held and, shortly afterwards, Collins received an anonymous telephone call suggesting that it mightn't be any harm if someone happened to leave the back gate unlocked.

And, as dusk folded its mantle about them, little groups began to stroll casually around the block and, finding the rear entrance to the plant invitingly ajar, they slipped inside and went about their work with souls technically unblemished by the mortal sin of picket-passing.

Next morning, the day shift again streamed from the buses. They too were now sadly conscious of the gaping wound in their paypackets and were resolved to stem the bleeding, even if it meant pulling the rug right from under the evening shift. When, however, they learned that the rug had already been pulled by their so-called comrades, and in such a shady manner, they were overcome with horror and rage.

'They're after bloody well sellin' us out,' someone remarked angrily.

'And they're supposed to be our friends,' added another.

'Friends how are ya!'

From there on, one heated comment led to another, and soon the angry epithets were being volleyed to and fro with ever-increasing vehemence and emotion.

'The dirty scabs,' a girl screamed.

'Blacklegs!' someone else howled.

'Cap'list feckin' stooges,' roared a male voice that sounded like Harry's.

'Good oul' Harry,' cried Peggy, in a shrill voice.

'Remember the Ardnaskeeha bus!' shouted Harry and that did it.

There was a great roar of approbation and support for Harry and his cause and emotion ran high and reason was laid low. And thus began Worldwide Electronics's first strike.

It was not exactly an all-out strike, since half of the employees supported Harry, while the other half continued to report to work. In the early stages, the two halves were never the same on any two consecutive days as loyalties, economic pressures or threats of mayhem caused individual participants to change sides without warning. But as the days passed, positions became more entrenched, attitudes more polarised, and minds more closed.

The Union official was unable to prolong the obsequies in Cork for as long as he would have wished and on the third day he appeared to the strikers. In no certain terms, he advised them that the strike was officially unofficial and that the Union could give them no support. In response, he was advised to go and get stuffed and he promptly made the strike official and tried to make overtures to the Company. Andrews, however, insisted that the strike was not only unofficial but unwarranted and that no talks would be held until everyone went back to work.

And so entrenchments were dug deeper and reason was declared redundant.

FOURTEEN

The company-sponsored disco was one of Andrews's limited family of brainchildren and was considered, at least by Andrews, to be a useful booster of employee morale and possibly even a subtle recruiting gimmick.

On the fourth Saturday of each month, Captain and his lady would take possession of Ballyderra's Community Hall and there set up a non-alcoholic bar and snack counter while their son, Kenny, the town's sole impresario, who drew the dole on the side, set up his portable disco and the local lads and lasses foregathered to have their eardrums pierced.

And so, on the last Saturday of August, the members of the Company's social committee not currently on strike met in conclave and, with unanimous grit, they determined that the show must go on, come what may.

At about the same time, Horny Harry reached his own unanimous decision to fight the good fight on all fronts, including the disco, even though it would entail the unprecedented measure of remaining sober on a Saturday night.

The disco was billed to start promptly at nine o'clock and the customers could be confidently counted upon to arrive shortly after eleven-thirty, when the law required the bars to close. But Harry was taking no chances and just before ten, armed with his formidable picket sign, he made his way towards the hall.

While he was still some distance off, the sound waves

sweeping out from Kenny's infernal machine struck his ears with force and he concluded, sadly, that the enemy had stolen a march on him.

The windows of the Community Hall were set high up and were very small so as to discourage gate-crashers and fresh air. But Harry was equal to the challenge. He propped his sign securely against the wall and climbed onto the crosspiece in order to survey the interior.

The sight that met his eyes was not entirely displeasing. He could see Captain, sprawled belly down across his counter in characteristically relaxed pose. Close at hand was Mrs Captain, eye-appealingly arranging her sandwiches and cakes. And, perched high up on the stage, Captain Junior peered with some difficulty through his orange coloured ringlets at the labels on his records. But unless one wished to count that trio, the hall was heartwarmingly devoid of human life.

Time passed and at eleven-thirty the girls began to arrive to be greeted by Harry's picket-brandishing figure. Even at the best of times, women are inconsistent creatures, guided by their feelings rather than their intellect. Get them committed to your cause, whatever it may be, and they will follow you to the death or worse. But obstruct their path when they are seductively geared up to put temptation in the way of the boys and they will most assuredly trample you into the dust.

And so, with typical female ruthlessness, the disco-hungry girls strolled past Harry, caring not a jot for the principles for which he stood or the horrible threats which he uttered.

A little later the boys began to show but they lacked the primal instincts of the girls and so they held back in grumbling, indecisive groups, safely out of reach of Harry's cruciform weapon. After a while, many of them went sadly back to the pubs because there were still places in Ballyderra where the licensing laws had never really caught on and sure they had to be doing something to keep them out of mischief on a Saturday night.

Only the more tenacious and the more randy ones hung in there, brooding dolefully on all that inaccessible girlflesh inside the hall. But even in the face of such cruel deprivation, none were so lacking in cowardice as to pass the dreaded sign.

Inside the hall the girls also were brooding on the indecisive boyflesh on the far side of Harry but, unlike the boys, they were prepared to do something about it.

Some of the more muscular ladies climbed onto stools and leaned invitingly through the side windows of the hall and the boys were not slow to get the message. Gradually, they trickled around the building to be quickly and sometimes painfully hauled upward and inward. By the time Harry realised what was going on it was too late for remedial action; the fellows and the girls were already whooping it up inside.

Once more Harry made a ladder from his sign and the sight that now met his eyes cut him to the very quick. Not only were they having a ball inside but, thanks to his sterling efforts, the boys were outnumbered two to one and that was surely a lovely way to go.

Harry consoled himself with the thought that tonight many of those girls would travel home without the satisfaction and fringe benefits of a male escort. But he realised that, in consequence, the boys were presented with a range of choice and golden opportunity greater than they had ever been exposed to before.

The thought was more than sex-starved flesh and blood could bear. Harry flung his sign violently beneath a nearby rosebush and marched belligerently into the hall. Strike or no strike, wasn't he a fully paid-up member of the social club and the Lord have mercy on anyone foolhardy enough to bar his way.

He elbowed his way through the smoke and the sound, squinting against the psychedelic lighting in search of a likely pair of knees and his expert eye quickly singled out the most appealing pair in the hall. They were over by the non-alcoholic bar, demurely tucked around the edge of a high stool and they belonged to the new girl, Imelda.

He strolled over and sat beside her, inspecting her tempting details from the corner of both eyes. She looked sad and wistful and his fingers itched to engulf those delectable knees in a comforting grip.

The record on Kenny's machine gave forth a dying scream and there was just time for a few intelligible words before the next one came to life.

'Will ya dance?' he enquired.

The fresh record erupted and she responded by smiling a little sadly and nodding.

For several minutes they squirmed about the floor, gazing vacantly into space, and then the music stopped again.

'Will ya have a drink?' he asked as they went back to their stools. She nodded and smiled and they managed to transmit their orders to Captain before the music struck again.

'You're kinda new here,' Harry yelled into her ear.

She nodded.

'What do you think of it?'

She smiled and shrugged one shapely shoulder, reserving judgment.

Harry wondered if she was always so sad.

What he did not know was that half an hour earlier, Imelda had devoured a large ice cream directly on top of a bag of somewhat oily potato chips, and her stomach was involved in a bitter altercation with the mixture. She hoped the Club Orange might act as an inner peacemaker.

They danced again, had another drink, danced, and had a drink and Imelda's stomach was not getting any better. Tiny beads of perspiration appeared on her smooth brow, and that was the opening that Harry needed.

"Tis awful hot in here,' he roared and she nodded.

'What about comin' out for a bit of air?' he suggested and he could not believe his luck when she nodded again.

They went out into the cool night air and he directed her around the hall and along the path behind the library.

There was one particular point where the side of the hall met the wall of the library next door and rose bushes had tucked themselves protectingly across the angle. Inside those bushes was a quiet and very private spot, well known to the young couples of Ballyderra. In fact, there was a locked brace already in occupancy. Harry greeted them warmly.

'Feck off oura that!' he suggested, and when they failed to move fast enough he added, 'Go on, or I'll tell the priest what ye were up to.'

The intimidated couple accepted Harry's advice and moved away, making hasty adjustments to their respective clothing.

It must be admitted that, up to this point, Harry had exercised admirable restraint but now, without warning, his biological motor went out of control. Ignoring the customary preliminaries, he grabbed Imelda in a bear-like embrace and backed her into the corner. He was now past the point of caring whether she screamed or kicked or gouged his eyes out. Come hell or high water, this was going to be his night to howl!

When Imelda neither screamed nor struggled, he was taken aback somewhat and had to pause briefly to rearrange his programme. Once he had accomplished this feat, he proceeded with the work in hand with determination and haste and it was not very long before the silence of the night was rent asunder by the agonised squeal from Harry's forcefully parted zipper.

'Ooooooh!' sighed Imelda and her stomach finally won the argument with the oily chips.

If anything can be guaranteed to put a man's fire out, it's

having the object of his attention get sick all over him, and even Horny Harry's bright glow was dimmed when the half-digested mixture struck him with force on the chest.

'Jawsus!' said he in some distress.

Instinctively he sprang back out of range, forgetting that there were rosebushes at his rear and that they were armed with long and very sharp thorns.

'Jawsus!' he commented once more as the thorns bit deep into his rear fender, causing him to leap forward again with even greater force.

It was Imelda's good fortune that she had moved to one side in the interim or Harry's forceful rebound would have left her permanently embedded in the library wall. And so it was the most forward protruding part of Harry that first struck the wall with a resounding thud, putting Harry's fire out for sure, and perhaps for keeps.

Showing a striking lack of consideration for her escort's plight, Imelda made a hasty withdrawal, leaving the poor man doubled over in agony, nursing his injured member and screaming blue, bloody murder.

It took a long time for the excruciating pain and Harry's howls to die down but finally he regained some of his composure. Calling loudly on every saint in the calendar to blast all women off the face of the earth, he uprooted some of the rank grass around the bushes and wiped down the front of his imitation leather jacket. Then, disconsolately, he retrieved his picket sign, slung it over his shoulder and minced painfully homeward.

As Harry passed by the labourers' cottages on the Limerick Road, Maudie Cahill happened to look out of her bedroom window and there she beheld a vision that stirred her soul to its very roots. There, against the night sky, she saw the pain-bowed figure, beard and all, with the cross over his shoulder and he making his way up the hill.

The good woman let out a howl fit to wake the dead and

took flight. Out of the house she sprinted and across the town with her long, grey hair and flowing flannel nightie streaming out behind her like a ship's wake and she never dropped anchor till she arrived at St John's presbytery.

She awakened the parish priest and his two curates and described to them vividly and breathlessly the vision she had just seen of Our Lord and he carrying his cross in the direction of Limerick.

They calmed her with stern words and some brandy and pointed out that it was two o'clock in the morning and would she please come back and give them the details at some more reasonable hour. The parish priest wrapped his coat around her so that she would not cause scandal to any innocents abroad at that ungodly hour, and they sent her on her way.

Maudie left the presbytery and streaked across the square, down to the quay, where she banged fervently on the studded door of the Friary until the reverend guardian and his community of five were gathered barefoot and heavy-eyed around her. Once more, she recounted her wondrous tidings.

They quieted her with soft invocations and a drink of cold water and sent her away with assurances that they would take the matter up with Rome at the earliest opportunity.

But Maudie's task was not yet completed. Further along the quay she trotted and woke the nuns in the Presentation Convent, who surrounded her in the chill hallway with devoutly chattering beads and teeth and told her to be sure and wake the nuns in the Mercy Convent, so that they too could share in the joyous tidings, which she duly did.

Then, in a state of physical and nervous prostration, Maudie returned home and the poor woman, who knew little of evil apart from her weekly bingo sessions, fell on her knees at her bedside and vowed that, till her dying day, if she lived that long, she would never sin again.

FIFTEEN

The voice on the phone was faint and tantalisingly familiar.

'Mr Collins,' it said, in a conversational tone, 'I just called to tell you there's an oul' bomb planted in the hostel an' 'tis set to go off in an hour.'

'All right' said Collins drowsily. 'Thanks for calling,' and he hung up and pulled the blankets up around his ears.

Lucy was wide awake and curious.

'Who was it?' she asked.

'Ah, nobody,' he told her as he snuggled back into the warm hollow he had just left.

Herself thought that over for a while, but no matter how she approached it, his answer seemed inadequate.

'How could it be no one,' she enquired, 'at three o'clock in the morning?'

'Just some nutcase.' Collins buried his face in the pillow, breathing sleep-deeply.

This answer was more acceptable and Lucy composed herself for slumber. But when her mind had femininely picked and poked at the matter for some minutes, she felt the need to pursue the subject further.

'What do you mean, a nutcase?' she demanded, and Collins came awake again with a sudden spasm.

– Dammit, can't a guy get some sleep –

'It can wait till the morning,' he said almost sharply.

As a rule, Collins knew better than to address his beloved in such churlish tones but the stresses of the strike, combined with the chafing of his enforced celibacy, were taking their toll on his normally peaceloving nature.

To give Lucy her due, she felt a certain sympathy for her harassed man, whom she loved dearly, and so she curbed her natural impulse to put him in his place with a few well-chosen words or a sudden cold spell. Besides, she reminded herself, he should be hearing shortly about the job with Leading Edge. And when decision time came, any minor tensions between them could distract him from the decision that she wanted him to believe was his to make.

She lay quietly, uncomplaining, for all of ten minutes, giving himself enough time to drift pleasantly back into oblivion. Then she sat violently upright, causing the bed to bounce lustily.

''Tis bad news!' she cried. 'That's why you won't tell me.'

– *Oh, shit* –

'Something happened to Mammy or Daddy!' she wailed.

– *Oh God, but pregnancy is hard on a man* –

'No!' said Collins.

'Auntie Kate got another stroke?'

'Will you go to sleep?' Collins pleaded.

'How can I sleep,' she demanded, 'when you won't tell me what's wrong?'

Collins sat up and glared at his lady, knowing that he could do so unscathed in the darkness.

'It was just some bloody nut,' he told her, 'calling to say there's a bomb planted in the hostel.'

Lucy considered this item of news for about five seconds.

'Why didn't you say so in the first place?' she demanded, and lay down and fell fast asleep.

Collins hoped that if he lay quite still and pondered on pleasant things, his vanished slumber might come sneaking back again.

– STOP THAT! –

His thoughts had started to wander over the new girl, Imelda.

– SIXTH: THOU SHALT NOT COMMIT ADULTERY –

– *Who's committing adultery?* –

– IMPURE THOUGHTS; MORTAL SINS –

– *Think about something else . . . this Transactional Analysis stuff . . . interesting* –

There was nothing very new about Transactional Analysis, but Collins had only just discovered it in one of his self-improvement books.

– *Yeah . . . let me see, now . . . everyone has three separate Ego states . . . Parent Ego, Child Ego, Adult Ego . . . We're in the Parent Ego when we lay down the law the things we learned from parents priests and teachers all the 'Thou shalts' and 'Thou shalt nots' . . . The Child Ego is when we're having fun following our emotions and feelings and being illogical or creative or destructive and then the Adult Ego is when we're being logical or reasoning The facts, ma'am . . . and when one person is in the Parent state and another is in the Adult, they're not communicating . . . what did they call it? Crossed transactions maybe like the conversations I have in my head . . . the little voice is my Child Ego and the big one is the Parent and my Adult Ego keeps getting stuck in between them . . . could be . . . but Imelda . . . Lord, she's really something I wonder is that the Child or the Adult Ego* –

– WATCH IT! –

– *Just thinking about the hostel girls in general* –

To prove his point he began to consider the courageous stand taken by the hostel girls in these dangerous, strike-shadowed days. Despite all threats and inducements, they showed up bravely for work each morning. Some might hint that their loyalty was prompted by the fact that their fixity of tenure in Company-owned accommodation might come unstuck if they downed tools, but there are always the begrudgers. And who could fault them for showing up late on Fridays when they clearly felt honour bound to join the pickets for an hour or so in order to collect a week's strike pay from the Union?

Suddenly, that telephone voice struck a familiar chord and the hirsute features of Horny Harry took shape in Collins's mind. With a few drinks in him, there was no telling what horrible vengeance that maniac might wreak on those picket-passing girls. He was, after all, a qualified craftsman, quite capable of manufacturing an infernal device to blow the hostel and its occupants, and possibly half of Ballyderra, to Kingdom Come.

– *Suffering Jesus* –

Collins felt the panic bubbling up from his lower gut like molten lava and gaining momentum as it travelled. With the ordeal of recruiting almost a hundred shift workers still fresh in his mind, the task of finding replacements for the hostel girls was a prospect too horrible to contemplate.

He got out of bed fast and telephoned the garda barracks.

The Ballyderra tennis club's annual dance had broken out at the Lakeside Hotel that night and some of the survivors, homeward bound, beheld a strange sight. On their unsteady way past the hostel, they were treated to the vision of a bevy of young ladies, and one not so young, huddled together on the lawn and clad in an eye-grabbing variety of night attire. Also present, towering protectively above them was Garda Superintendent Merry, in a foul mood at being disturbed in the middle of the night. Behind the Superintendent trailed his gallant little band of men, Sergeant O'Meara, and Gardaí O'Shaughnessy and Kennedy, clad in varying stages of blue uniformity. There, too, was the well-built figure of Brian Collins, with his green and gold pyjama legs inching down below his trouser cuffs.

The revellers pressed against the tall railings and

speculated on the cause of the disturbance, hoping that it was an orgy of some kind and that they might be allowed to partake.

The Superintendent approached the onlookers and suggested that they clear off to hell about their business but his words, though delivered with force, had little effect.

Sergeant O'Meara, wise in the ways of people, strolled to the edge of the gathering and remarked causally that there was a bomb on the premises and it might go off at any moment and, as the word rustled through the crowd like a fresh summer breeze, they decided jointly and severally that the Superintendent's advice was good. The audience filtered away into the darkness.

Doc Roche, the Company's physician, part-time, arrived at a trot and the Superintendent told him to stand by to give aid, but Doc was not one to remain idle for long in such opportune conditions. Soon he was passing among the huddled girls administering words of comfort and reassuring pats on carefully selected targets.

Horny Harry appeared out of nowhere and he, too, went among the girls, patting them with an anatomical selectivity that was at least equal to Doc's. Collins turned a highly suspicious eye on Harry but, considering the legal and physical consequences of tossing accusations about, he decided to keep his own counsel.

Collins and the Superintendent went into hasty conclave with Miss Henderson, who was busily counting and recounting the heads of her protégées.

Miss Henderson was in her early fifties, small and grey, trim and prim, and occupied the front downstairs flat in the hostel. She was employed by the Company to oversee the domestic and social activities of the young ladies and to defend their morals against all comers, which she did with great energy and venom.

'Look, Miss Henderson,' the Superintendent was

115

arguing, 'those girls must be moved out of the grounds.'

'If you think for one moment,' snapped Miss Henderson, 'that I'm going to allow my girls out on the street in their night clothes – ' The thought struck her dumb, but only for a moment. 'Never!' she cried, 'Never!'

'There could be a bomb inside there,' Collins argued.

'Woe to the scandal giver!' exclaimed Miss Henderson apropos of something or other.

'They could get killed,' the Superintendent pointed out.

'There are worse fates,' said the lady, and the Super-intendent conceded defeat.

'All right then,' he said, 'get them back behind that wall.' He pointed to a partly demolished shed at the far end of the garden and Doc and Miss Henderson herded the scantily-clad girls towards shelter with Horny Harry patting the strays on the flanks.

Then the Superintendent marshalled his troops.

'We're going in,' he announced and was greeted with a most articulate silence.

'Aren't we going to wait for the bomb experts from Limerick?' enquired Sergeant O'Meara.

'We can be searching while we're waiting,' the Super-intendent informed him, impatient to get back to his warm bed.

'When is it due to go off?' Malone asked Collins.

Collins peered at his luminous watch.

'In about half an hour.'

'I have no intention of forcing anyone against his will,' the Superintendent reassured his men. 'I'm just asking for volunteers. Anyone who hasn't the guts for it can go and hide behind the wall with the rest of the women.'

Put like that, it was difficult to refrain from volunteering and the gallant band went inside to search.

'We'll pray for you,' Miss Henderson called encouragingly after them as she got her protégées behind the wall, shivering with cold and excitement.

'Now girls,' she announced, 'we'll say the Rosary.'

But Doc was too quick for her. He had quite a good tenor voice and an extensive repertoire and soon he had the girls singing their way through a non-stop succession of sad airs and fiery ballads and bawdy love songs, while Miss Henderson prayed fervently and alone.

When the squad car arrived from Limerick the experts were instantly drawn towards the siren scene at the bottom of the garden. However, they were brought quickly back to reality by a bull-like roar from the Superintendent and they dashed inside to add their expertise to the search.

Harry got his face convincingly slapped for the second time and he transferred his attentions to another quarter. Miss Henderson went smoothly from the Rosary to the Litany for the Dead, while the Doc began a plaintive solo performance of 'The Lark in the Clear Air'.

However, by now the first fever of excitement had begun to wane and the cold night air started to percolate through flimsy nighties. Goose bumps made their presence felt on delicate bodies and the chattering of teeth was heard above the singing.

'What time is it?' asked one of the girls.

Collins checked his watch. It was ten after four. The explosion was already ten minutes overdue.

'Bomb or no bomb,' exclaimed the girl who had spoken, 'I amn't going to stay out here and catch me death of cold. I'm going back to me bloody bed.'

The motion was carried unanimously and, despite protestations from Collins and Doc, the girls marched back to the house. On the high steps before the entrance they paused and their leader spoke.

'Mr Collins,' she said, 'this was a call-out.'

'What?' asked Collins, puzzled.

'Call-out,' the girl repeated. 'The Union agreement

117

says we get a minimum of three hours pay at time and a half for a call-out.'

For the life of him, Collins could not summon up an appropriate reply.

"Tis four hours at double time after midnight,' another girl amended.

'You're right then, Janie,' said the spokeswoman, 'and the same amount of time off with pay in the morning.'

'This isn't a call-out,' Collins argued lamely.

'We were called out, weren't we?'

'All right,' said Collins, stalling, 'we'll discuss it in the morning.'

'Sure,' said the girl, 'any time after twelve.'

Twenty-six heads nodded in solid support and they bustled back into the hostel. Without the slightest concern for the inconvenience and palpitations they were causing the searchers, the girls settled once more into their respective beds.

Some time later the experts were obliged to declare the place safe and bomb-free and they took their leave, some of their number casting longing, lingering looks behind.

SIXTEEN

There were many devout people in the organisation who believed that Philip de Briggi reported direct to God, but the real old hands knew better. After all, wasn't he President, Chief Executive and Chairman of the Board; three divine persons all rolled into one. In their book, he *was* God!

And in just one week, the great man would appear before his Irish flock to impart his blessing on the Model 660. To have his apparition greeted by picketing strikers was an unthinkable blasphemy and so the transatlantic fax spewed out messages which daily grew more insistent.

'Settle!' they demanded. 'Settle, so that our leader may come and go in serenity, or human sacrifice will be called for.'

Around Jennifer Carey's fax-strewn conference table, her staff meeting was in full cry, seeking an out that might have so far eluded their collective brainstorms.

'We gotta do something,' suggested Haley forcefully and the statement was so all-embracing that no reply could do it justice.

'We can't give in!' cried Andrews, angrily defensive. 'We'd lose face.'

'Better than losing our asses,' O'Shee snapped, 'and that's just what we're doing.' There was a slight pause. 'Jesus,' he exploded, 'the 660 project is dead in its tracks.'

'Do you have any suggestions?' J. J. asked.

'Sure I have,' said O'Shee. 'Settle and let's get back on

stream.'

'Settle on what terms?' Andrews enquired.

'Whatever you can get, for Chrissakes.'

'Look,' said Andrews, making a great effort to stay smilingly calm, 'we disciplined the guy in accordance with the agreed procedure. He then goes on a one-man unofficial strike, which is contrary to all accepted procedures. Then the Union makes it official, and no procedure can allow . . .'

'Shove your goddam procedures!' roared O'Shee, who hated all Personnel people with a deep and abiding passion and didn't care who knew it.

'I'll put the question one more time,' said J. J. quietly. 'Does anyone have any concrete suggestions?'

'Get rid of the whole goddam Personnel department,' O'Shee proposed.

J. J. turned her large grey-green eyes on each of her henchmen in turn, but it was obvious that no practicable suggestions were forthcoming.

'Very well,' she said, 'unfortunately time is against us. Therefore, I see only one course of action open to us. And that is to reinstate the guy and get the strike called off.'

'Endorsed,' said O'Shee with satisfaction.

The smile dribbled down Andrews's chin.

'We can't!' he exclaimed. 'That would be total capitulation.'

'Give me an alternative,' J. J. asked.

'Stand firm. They'll give in eventually.'

'Eventually is too late,' J. J. insisted. 'Mr de Briggi arrives next week.'

'What about the girls on line one?' Andrews argued.

'What about them?'

'They threatened to strike if we didn't get rid of the guy.'

'Hell,' said O'Shee, 'they only say things like that to scare the shit out of Personnel.'

'It would be seen,' Andrews pointed out, 'as an admission that we were wrong in the first place.'

'Maybe,' suggested O'Shee, pointedly, 'someone *was* wrong,' and that remark automatically led the meeting into the time-honoured exercise of find-a-fall-guy.

When Doc Roche reported to the Medical Centre, he found an unusual note on his desk. It was neatly written on a page torn from a pocket diary, and it said,

> Dear Doctor,
> We are all terrible worried over Imelda Heffernan and you should give her a complete examination because we think she has a medical problem. If you don't, we will all leave the hostel.
> Signed:
> Worried Hostel Girls

Doc Roche did not hold with anonymous letters. On the other hand, the prospect of examining Imelda was not at all to his disliking.

'Nurse Flynn,' he called, and the dimpled knees came bobbing in in quick succession.

'What do you think of that?' Doc handed her the note.

Dimpleknees read and shrugged her starched bosom.

'If you ask me,' she said, ''tis someone with a grudge against her.'

'You're probably right,' he agreed, then added craftily. 'on the other hand, they're threatening to leave the hostel.'

'That makes it a matter for Personnel,' Dimpleknees suggested.

Doc pretended to consider the suggestion.

'You're right,' he said, 'but you know Personnel. They'll probably say it's a medical matter and pass the buck right back to us.'

'They probably would,' she agreed, and Doc pressed home his advantage.

'Besides,' he argued, 'if the poor girl is really not well, we'd be neglecting our duty.'

'That's true,' said the nurse. 'You ought to examine her.'

'Whatever you say,' agreed Doc.

Collins was sitting in his office, observing the gyrations of the pickets outside, when Doc appeared perspiring before him.

'Brian,' said the Doc, visibly shaking, 'I'm afraid we have a serious problem.'

'Who're you telling?' Collins asked, still looking through the window.

''Tis about Imelda. Imelda Heffernan.'

'What about her?' Collins asked, showing a little more interest.

'She's suffering from . . . ' Doc couldn't bring himself to utter the dreaded word, 'a serious social disease.'

'What does that mean?'

'Highly contagious . . . to men.'

Collins still looked puzzled.

'VD, man,' Doc snapped impatiently.

– Holy Christ –

'Holy Christ!' Collins remarked.

'You'll have to get her out of here quick,' Doc urged, 'before she does serious damage.'

– Too late –

Collins had been hearing some interesting reports about Imelda's strong inclination towards nymphomania but his Adult Ego had dismissed them as wishful thinking on the part of the reporters. Now his Parent Ego took over and he grabbed the phone and violently dialled Reverend Father Keenan's number.

'Father Keenan,' he yelled into the phone, 'this is Brian Collins.'

'Hello Brian,' said the priest cheerfully.

'I'm calling about Imelda Heffernan.'

'Oh yes?' the holy man's voice sounded a little farther away. 'How's she getting on?'

'You'll have to come and take her away.'

'What's the matter?' asked the priest.

'She's suffering from a serious social disease,' Collins told him, 'highly contagious to men.'

'Good Heavens!' exclaimed Father Keenan.

'Can you come and take her away?'

'I have confessions all day today.'

'I'll send her home in a taxi so,' Collins offered.

Father Keenan realised he was boxed in. He had been only too well aware of the spiritual havoc wrought by Imelda among the menfolk of Ardnaskeeha. Now he was learning that their bodies might be in as much danger as their souls. The last thing he wanted was to see her return to spread ruination among those that she hadn't yet got around to, if any. And so Ardnaskeeha's penitents were left unshriven that day, while Father Keenan collected Imelda and continued on to Limerick in search of medical treatment, alternative employment or concealment, or all of the above.

The partitioning around Collins's office was far from soundproof, and he had been too agitated during his conversation with Father Keenan to observe reasonable precautions. As a result, Liz Donovan developed a pressing need to adjourn to the ladies' room in search of an audience.

In normal circumstances, a snippet of confidential scandal took upward of an hour to reach every ear in the plant, but this item broke all records and within twenty minutes people were passing the word to those who already knew.

Doc spent a while in conversation with Collins trying to calm both their nerves and by the time he returned to his surgery there was a long line of potential patients awaiting his ministrations. All males, and all remarking loudly and hoarsely on how suddenly these summer colds could strike a man down. Collins looked out at the picket. Five men, six young ladies on parade. Among them his cousin P. J. McMahon, sheepishly holding up a sign with the words 'Official Strike' boldly printed across it.

P. J. played left half forward for the county hurling team and had some political aspirations, so you couldn't really blame him for going along with the strikers.

– Maybe you'd be better off to take that job in Dublin –

– WHO SAYS YOU'LL GET IT? *–*

– Will you look at poor P. J. out there he'd rather be in here doing his job but what can he do a member of the Labour Party and all wait a minute didn't you see him the other night in his battered old Fiat driving up towards the Mountain Road Imelda in the passenger seat . . . God, supposing –

Collins proceeded to suppose the worst.

– YOU'D BETTER GET OUT THERE AND WARN HIM *–*

– We can't compromise the Company's position by talking to them –

– SO YOU'RE GOING TO LET YOUR COUSIN GO DOWN WITH THE POX! *–*

Harry was the first to see Collins bearing down on the picket line.

'Hah!' he roared triumphantly. 'They're givin' in.'

Collins halted several yards away.

'P. J.' he called, 'can I talk to you a minute?'

P. J. looked uncomfortable as he became the focal point of all eyes.

'Don't go near him,' Harry warned. 'He's tryin' to intimate ya.'

P. J. looked from Collins to Harry and back again.

'It's a personal matter,' Collins told them. 'It has nothing to do with the dispute.'

'Ya expect us ta believe that bullshit?' Harry enquired.

Collins looked as earnestly as he could at his cousin.

'It's important, P. J.,' he said. 'Trust me.'

P. J. nodded and walked over to Collins.

'Don't listen ta that cap'list stooge,' Harry warned.

Under the watchful gaze of the picketers, Collins spoke swiftly and softly and P. J.'s normally rosy cheeks were seen to lose their colour rapidly.

'What the hell!' Andrews exclaimed.

His position at the conference table enabled him to keep a weather eye on the picket outside, and there was his right hand man out there talking to one of the strikers.

Jennifer Carey and the rest of her staff reacted to Andrews's alarm and gathered around the window.

'What's that guy doing?' J. J. demanded.

'He's not supposed to talk to them!' Andrews groaned, 'He's compromising our position.'

They watched in silence for a moment in a tight little group as Collins continued his chat with P. J.. Then J. J. turned back to the table.

'OK,' she said, 'let's get on with the business in hand. But,' she stared steadily at Andrews, 'I'll want a full explanation of what's going on out there.'

'You'll get it,' Andrews promised. 'If he's made any kind of overtures to them, he's in deep shit.'

P. J., still ashen-faced, turned back to his fellow strikers as Collins departed, his good deed done.

'Well?' Harry demanded. 'What was he on about?'

P. J. was an honest and direct young man and he felt obliged to pass on the information about Imelda. And, as he did, a number of other faces also began to lose their colour.

For his part, Harry offered up silent thanks to his patron

saint that the proceedings behind the library on the night of the disco had so rudely been cut short. He noted that a number of his fellow strikers hastily dropped their signs and headed for the medical centre and he wondered how far *they'd* got. Then, uneasily, he began to wonder how far it took and, despite his calm and logical self-assurances that he had nothing to fear, he began to work himself rapidly into a state of terror.

'Jawsus!' said he explosively and, laying down his cross, he followed the other defectors inside.

Examining the male anatomy held very little appeal for Doc and by the time he had inspected, dosed and advised twenty-two very worried men he was feeling quite depressed, though he could not but wonder at the enthusiasm and stamina of a girl who could cover so much territory in such a short time.

Horny Harry was number twenty-three and he was even more bashful than his predecessors. He sidled in, uneasy, uncertain and loath to confess to his misdeed.

'Well?' snapped Doc as Harry stood there with one hand as long as the other.

'I have a sore throat,' said Harry, feigning huskiness.

'A sore throat?' Doc asked sceptically and Harry nodded.

'Are you sure 'tis your throat that's sore?' Doc gave him an opening but Harry could only nod faintheartedly.

'All right,' said Doc, 'open your mouth.'

Doc flashed a light into Harry's mouth and stuck a lollipop stick back among his tonsils.

'There's no inflammation,' Doc pronounced. 'Are you absolutely sure it's your throat?'

By this stage Harry's courage had totally deserted him and he gagged affirmatively.

Doc began to press the glands around Harry's neck and every time he asked if it hurt, Harry nodded, which further increased Doc's confusion.

'I'd better take a saliva sample,' Doc said, for want of a constructive idea. He handed Harry a test tube.

'Expectorate into that,' he said as he turned to his physiology manual in search of inspiration. He looked up quickly when he heard the buzz of a zipper.

'I said spit, not piss!' he roared but he was too late. Harry was in full spate.

All through the long morning the unfortunate man had badly needed to go but he was not one to desert his post under pressure, even from his bladder. Now that he was in full motion, there was no way of turning him off and, unfortunately, his capacity far exceeded that of the test tube.

Wildly, he looked around for a receptacle to take the surplus and he spied the lid of a waste bin peeping from beneath the desk. He made a dash in that direction, weaving an intricate pattern on the floor and part way up the wall. To his dismay, he found that his target was made of open weave and quite useless for his purpose.

'The sink, you fool,' screamed Doc and Harry spun nimbly towards the small sink in the corner. On the turn, he caught Doc in the line of fire and left his mark on the little man's trouser legs. By the time he reached the sink his resources had run dry and, for a time, he stood there sadly, with head hanging, surveying the innocent-looking source of all that destruction.

'You stupid, bloody half-wit!' Doc screamed at him. 'Get out of my surgery!'

For all his superior size, Harry quailed before the Doc's rage and he retreated in disarray. His passage through the production area aroused some interest because, in his confusion, he had omitted to put everything back in its proper place. He made his way out of the building, paying no heed to the screams of delighted shock that followed him.

On the lawn outside, he found the picket signs stacked

like the weapons of a surrendered army but of his faithful followers not one remained. This, on top of the cloud that now hung over his manliness, was just too much. Harry went in search of solace to the nearest pub.

Back in the Medical Centre, Doc surveyed the examination room and decided to declare it a disaster area.

'Nurse,' he bawled, and Dimpleknees appeared. She stopped short at the sight that met her limpid eyes. She inspected the intricate designs on the wall and floor. She noted the little cascades descending from the desk top. Then she spied the damaged front of Doc's trousers.

'Holy Mother of Jesus!' she exclaimed, and ran out of the place.

Doc grabbed the phone by the throat and dialled maintenance.

'Foley here,' the phone said.

'This is an emergency,' Doc announced. 'Get someone up to the Medical Centre to clean it up.'

He hung up before Foley could open a discussion on the nature of the emergency and the need for a work order in triplicate. Then he picked up his newspaper and, holding it casually draped down his front, he walked with dignity, if a little stiff-legged, out of the plant.

The meeting in J. J.'s office had reached a verdict. After all, who had precipitated the strike in the first place by suspending Harry without fully considering the potential adverse consequences? Who had failed to give the defendant the opportunity to present his case through the grievance procedure? And whose ill-advised action had already cost the company many thousands of dollars in lost output?

By acclamation and *in absentia*, Collins was elected the sacrificial offering. Andrews, to give him due credit, raised some objections, but long experience in similar situations

128

had taught him that the fall guy inevitably came from Personnel and, since that narrowed the field to Collins or himself, he allowed his objections to be overruled without too much of a struggle.

Andrews was directed to administer a severe reprimand to Collins, get him to call the Union and tell them that Harry would be reinstated without loss of pay and let the Union stomp all over him if they felt so inclined. It was a small price to pay to make sure that Mr de Briggi's delicate senses would not be assailed by the sight of picket-bearing employees.

With that little matter effectively resolved, the meeting got down to the more serious business of preparing for de Briggi's visit.

It was obvious to all that there was now no hope of getting the 660 line up to speed in time for the de Briggi visitation, and O'Shee was instructed to set up a simulated production line. It would not fool their beloved President, but he would appreciate the need to deceive the invited representatives of Church, State and Press. The label on the sample which J. J. had on ice would be surreptitiously changed, and it would be presented before all concerned as the first Irish-assembled Model 660, and who the hell would know the difference.

Andrews was appointed coordinator of festivities and was directed to choose an organising committee of energetic employees who would not be greatly missed from their normal duties, and to use them as he saw fit.

Planning was to be of the essence. No expense was to be spared. And no foul-ups would be tolerated.

As the meeting rose to adjourn, J. J. happened to glance out the window.

Jesus!' she remarked, 'What the hell is going on now?'

They gathered together and looked in puzzlement at the picketless roadway outside.

'Find out what they're up to,' J. J. snapped and Andrews

got Collins on the phone.

'What the hell is going on?' he demanded.

'What do you mean, Merv?' asked Collins, a little too innocently.

'Where are the pickets?' Andrews asked.

'Gone back to work.'

'Gone back to work?' Andrews repeated incredulously, and J. J. grabbed the phone from him.

'J. J. here,' she said, 'what concessions did you make?'

'Concessions?' Collins asked. 'There were no concessions.'

'I saw you out there talking to them.'

'Oh, yes.'

– *Get yourself some kudos out of this* –

– Where's all this integrity! –

'That was just a personal thing,' Collins said. 'One of the picketers is my cousin and I needed to give him an urgent message.'

'You must have had something to do with it, Brian.'

– *At least take* some *credit* –

'Not really,' said Collins, trying to sound noticeably modest. 'Not really.'

'And you made no concessions?'

'Not a thing, Miz Carey . . . '

'Hell. Call me J. J . I'll want you to give me the details later. Well done, Brian.'

J. J. hung up and turned to her bemused team.

'You know,' she remarked, 'I have a feeling we may have underrated Collins. I believe he may have real growth potential.' And Andrews began to feel a little sick, because the next time a fall guy was needed, Collins's potential might be allowed to grow right over him.

SEVENTEEN

Ned Barry, the Union's branch secretary, was an intense and overweight young man who was destined for high places in the brotherhood and well on his way to his first duodenal ulcer. As a professional proletarian, he shunned the use of tie or jacket and favoured navy polo-necked sweaters and unpressed denim trousers. The news that tools had been upped at the plant made a significant contribution to the progress of his ulcer and, breathless with indignation, he clocked out from his job with the Council. He squeezed his potbelly behind the wheel of his decomposing Fiesta and drove at high speed to the plant.

Sure enough, the picket was gone. He waddled perspiringly inside and demanded immediate audience with Collins.

'Take a seat, Ned,' Collins invited smugly.

Ned ignored the courtesy and pressed his frontage belligerently against the desk.

'What are yez up to now?' he enquired aggressively.

'What do you mean?' Collins asked.

– Don't gloat you'll only get him mad –

'Where's our pickets? What kind of fuckin' tricks are yez tryin' to pull?' Ned began to pound his large fist on the desk.

– He's into Child Ego –

'No tricks,' Collins assured him, 'they downed signs just as suddenly as they downed tools.'

'Where are they gone to?'

131

'Back to work, where else?'

—That would be your Adult Ego —

— STOP PLAYING GAMES —

Ned began to breathe heavily through his nose and his face turned a coronary red.

'I demand to see Harry,' he snarled.

'Harry isn't here.'

'Where is he, so?'

Collins shook his head.

'He came into the Medical Centre a while ago and then he took off for points unknown.'

'Yez made a deal with the treacherous bastard,' Ned accused. 'Yez bought the hoor off.'

'Honest to God, Ned. We didn't.'

— Crossed transactions . . . communications breakdown —

'I'll find out,' Ned shouted, further stoking the embers of his ulcer, 'and when I do, yez won't know what hit yez.'

'He's probably in some pub getting stoned,' Collins suggested helpfully.

— And that's probably your Child Ego —

It took Ned three days to run Harry to earth and a fourth to sober him up, after which they arrived at the plant, breathing fire and alcohol fumes and seeking instant access to Collins.

Collins knew that, for discussions of such a delicate nature, it was desirable to have a witness in attendance and, in the present situation, one who could double as a bodyguard might be in order. He called Andrews who sidestepped with admirable agility and suggested that Harry's supervisor, Foley, would be more appropriate. Foley was small and quick on his feet and could be confidently counted on to take to the hills at the first sign of trouble. A witness he might be, a bodyguard he was not, but Collins had little choice.

And so they gathered around Collins's desk, Ned with fire in his belly, Harry with fire in his head, and Foley poised strategically convenient to the door.

'Well?' asked Collins to get the ball rolling.

'We're here about Comrade Harry,' Ned announced.

'What about him?' Collins asked.

'We want to know his present status.'

'What do you mean, status?'

'Is he sacked?'

'Of course not,' Collins assured them.

'You mean,' Ned asked incredulously, 'you want him back?'

Collins smiled, savouring the situation.

'We didn't fire him,' he explained. 'He quit.'

With some difficulty, Harry raised his head.

'I never quit,' he croaked.

Collins held up the pocket size Union agreement.

'Section six subsection two of the agreement says and I quote,' Collins quoted, all in one breath. 'Any employee who is absent for two or more consecutive days and who fails to notify the Company within that time of the cause and likely duration of the absence, shall be deemed to have voluntarily terminated his employment. Which means,' Collins translated for Harry, 'you quit.'

'There was a strike on,' Ned argued.

'Yes, but it ended four days ago.'

'That's downright unreasonable,' Ned complained.

'It's in the agreement.'

'How could he call in and he too bloody drunk – too sick,' Ned amended hastily.

'It's in the agreement,' Collins maintained and Ned changed his approach.

'Look!' he said reasonably to Collins, 'Could the two of us talk this over in private?'

'Certainly,' said Collins, and Foley and Harry withdrew.

'Now,' said Ned conspiratorially, 'you and me have worked well together over the years, considering everything. Haven't we now?' His patent sincerity put Collins instantly on his guard.

'We certainly have,' he agreed with equal conviction.

'Well, do us a favour and take Harry back.'

'You're joking.'

'To tell yez the truth,' Ned confided, 'the crowd above in headquarters are doing their nut about this whole bloody thing. If yez take him back, 'twill get them offa my neck.'

Collins shook his head slowly.

'We're damn lucky to be rid of him,' he said.

'I know bloody well yez are,' Ned agreed, 'but couldn't yez take him back and give me the credit for it. Sure he'll be grabbin' the girls again in no time and the minute he does you can fire him proper.'

'And,' said Collins, 'the strike would start all over again.'

'After all the trouble he's after causin' me!' exclaimed the Union man, 'I own to God if yez wanted to crucify the hoor, I'd hand yez the nails.'

Collins continued to shake his head.

'The risk would be too great,' he said, and Ned's bile began to warm up once again.

'Yez mean yez won't cooperate,' he shouted.

– *More crossed transactions* –

'I can't.'

'All right then,' Ned flung the door open to re-admit Harry. 'Yez are askin' for trouble.' Foley remained safely outside.

'I should have known,' Ned now addressed Harry, ''tis a waste of time talkin' to this crowd. What do they care about the rights of the individual?' He raised his voice so that his performance would be appreciated in the neighbouring offices. 'Exploiting the workers. Never give a shite about the little man. That's the way with them.'

'They won't take me back?' Harry enquired.

134

'They aren't going to get away with it,' Ned assured him. 'The Union will see that your rights are protected.'

'They can shove their feckin' job,' Harry responded. 'I wouldn't work for them if I was dyin' of the thirst.'

'I suppose,' Ned said to him nastily, 'you think you can go and draw unemployment for yourself.'

'Why shouldn't I?' Harry demanded, 'I paid enough into it.'

'That doesn't mean you'll get anything back out of it,' said Ned with a sneer.

'I feckin' well will,' said Harry.

Ned turned to Collins.

'Did yez send his form to the Unemployment Office?' he asked.

'Posted it yesterday.' Collins hadn't missed a trick.

– Put that in your pipe and smoke it says my Child Ego –

'And what did yez put down,' Ned enquired, 'as his reason for leaving?'

'What the procedure says,' Collins told him. 'Left of his own accord.'

Ned grinned with happy malice and turned to Harry.

'What did I tell yez?' he asked. 'They don't give a shite about the little man.'

'What do you mean?' Harry asked.

'They told the unemployment exchange that yez quit,' Ned pointed out, 'they don't pay unemployment if yez quit. Yez have to be fired.'

'Jawsus!' said Harry, beginning to comprehend.

'That's their way of getting back at a fella,' Ned said, 'they'd take the bite out of your mouth.'

Harry was halfway across the desk, going for Collins's throat and Foley was already in full flight when Ned intervened.

'Don't play into their hands,' he shouted, hauling Harry off Collins. 'There's other ways of dealing with them.'

'I'll burn the feckin' place down,' Harry promised, 'if ye

135

don't fire me.'

'We can't fire you,' Collins told him calmly. 'You already quit.'

'I think,' suggested Ned, 'we better talk alone again.' And, with an effort, he ushered Harry out of the office.

'Come on now,' Ned pleaded with Collins, 'the least yez can do is take the hoor back so that you can fire him.'

'I tell you,' Collins insisted, 'we can't take the risk.'

'Just to let him get his unemployment.'

'Nothing doing,' Collins said firmly.

'We'll take it to the Labour Court,' Ned threatened.

Collins shrugged his shoulders and Ned abandoned the reasonable approach again.

'All right then,' he shouted. 'We tried to be reasonable, but yez refused to listen. We'll have yez up for unfair dismissal.'

'We followed the rules to the letter,' Collins insisted.

'But there were extenuating circumstances,' Ned shouted.

'What extenuating circumstances?'

'How the hell do I know?' Ned told him. 'But we'll think of some, never fear.' And on that note he left the premises, closely attended by Horny Harry.

EIGHTEEN

Lunch in the Lakeside Hotel had consisted of reasonably presentable roast lamb with mixed vegetables, accompanied by the blandest of small talk. Now was time for coffee and some serious plotting.

The man seated across the table from Jennifer J. Carey was tall, lean and self-assured. His dark grey suit was obviously American and expensive as befitted the exalted position of Vice-President of International Operations. His name was Fred M. Williams and he was Miz Carey's immediate boss. He was also a man with a keen liking for the opposite gender and with a sizeable yen for his subordinate in particular.

Miz Carey, in turn, was well aware of her boss's dishonourable intentions towards her and she hoped that some day he would yield to the temptation and give her the opportunity to lay the sexist bastard low with a knee in the you-know-whats, closely followed by a sexual harrassment suit.

Williams swept the dining room with a wary eye. They were the only customers in the place, but he had a sensitivity to industrial espionage that bordered on the neurotic and the items on his after-lunch agenda could be of value to enemies, inside or outside the Company.

'Let's have our coffee out in the garden,' Williams suggested.

They seated themselves gingerly on wrought-iron chairs, painted white among the rhododendrons in the garden.

Between them was a small round wrought-iron table, also white, and, like the chairs, slightly unsteady on its feet.

'Now, about the strike, J. J.,' Williams opened the proceedings in hushed tones.

'Yeah,' said J. J. ruefully.

'Hey don't look so glum,' Williams consoled her. 'You know our slogan: "There are no problems, only opportunities!"' He paused and let that pearl of wisdom hang in the air for a moment.

'And I'm happy to inform you that we're off the hook over that goddam strike.' Williams looked around to make sure no one was within earshot. 'It helped us solve a serious inventory problem.'

He went on to explain to his subordinate how the Marketing Division's sales forecasts had been way off the mark (so what's new!) and that Production Planning had been dumb enough to believe those forecasts. The result had been that Model Ks had flowed into stores much faster than they had flowed out into the market and inventories in the US had piled up to an uneconomically embarrassing level. The work stoppage in Ireland couldn't have come at a better time. It had given them a chance to get the inventories nicely depleted.

'De Briggi has actually managed to convince the Board that we planned the whole thing,' Williams said 'and, in the process, I think he convinced himself as well ... So,' he concluded, 'we're smelling like a rose. And we got Marketing and Production Planning out of the deep shit so they owe us big.'

J. J. nodded and smiled. What had looked like a major diversion on her career path might now be turned into a shortcut.

'So,' continued Williams, 'if de Briggi brings up the subject, do what you can to reinforce the belief. Short of telling a direct lie, of course.' (That we could get caught out on, he added to himself.)

J. J. nodded thoughtfully. She decided to avoid confirming or denying anything, if de Briggi happened to ask.

'Now. Another big item.' Williams paused as a nubile young lady approached. She was squeezed into traditional waitress garb of black dress and white, frilly apron that did her tempting form more than justice. As she bent over to set the coffee jug and cups carefully on the table, Williams helped himself to a lecherous eyeful.

'Watch that oul' table,' she warned them, ''twill topple over on yere laps if ye aren't careful.'

Williams waited until she was out of earshot and speculative eyeball before he picked up the conversation again.

'Let me ask you something, J. J.,' Williams said. 'How would you feel about staying on here for an extra few years?'

'Not very happy!' said J. J. with conviction. 'I only took this job on the understanding that I'd be transferred back to headquarters after three years.'

'Wait till you hear my proposition,' said Williams, smiling. 'At this moment in time, we're negotiating the takeover of a manufacturing operation in Spain. They produce printed circuit boards, capacitors, resistors, semi-conductors. They have a lot of technical know-how we could use, but they're piss-poor on the business end. We think we can get it real cheap.'

'Vertical integration,' said J. J. non-committally. 'Sounds like a good idea.'

'Actually de Briggi and I are heading for Spain straight after the ceremonies here,' Williams went on. 'We hope to have the whole deal wrapped up in less than a month.'

J. J. poured coffee into both cups.

'You take cream or sugar?' she asked.

Williams shook his head and picked up his cup.

'So,' Williams sipped his coffee without any great relish, 'the question is: how would you like to run both operations from here?'

'Both operations?'

Williams nodded. He knew he had his audience's full attention now.

'Yeah,' he said. 'The exposure you have gained in an underdeveloped country like this would be invaluable in Spain. And it would certainly broaden your experience.'

The idea was interesting, but J. J. knew that the less enthusiasm she showed the better the package she could negotiate. She shook her head.

'I've been out of the mainstream for three years already,' she pointed out. 'I need some exposure back at headquarters. Otherwise I'll be overlooked for any opportunities.'

'Damn it, lady. This *is* exposure. This is one hell of an opportunity for you.'

'It would still keep me out on the boondocks.'

'I wouldn't consider the job of Vice-President, West Europe Operations as being out in the boondocks.'

J. J. was a good poker player, but it took an extra effort to hide her heightened interest in the exalted title. The Company's first woman vice-president. Wouldn't that be something!

'And, of course, there will be a Company apartment at your disposal for your trips to Madrid.'

'Let me think about it.'

'De Briggi will probably bring it up with you when he arrives tomorrow,' Williams said. 'How about having a decision by then?'

'We'll see.'

They moved on to a discussion of the programme for de Briggi's impending arrival.

Philip de Briggi hovered in the sky above the plant and tried to read his *Wall Street Journal* in the cramped confines of the helicopter cabin.

Someone with nothing better to do had calculated that the average height of CEOs of major multinational companies

140

was six foot and half an inch. Which meant that, somewhere in corporate America, there had to be a six-foot-six-inch chief executive to offset de Briggi's five foot seven. He was a broad man, whichever way you measured him, solid, rather than fat, and he carried his short-cropped head in an aggressive forward thrust. His face was dark and battered, more like a Mafia enforcer than a businessman. He had a most striking nose, large, flattened and with a pronounced list to starboard. Rumour had it that its unnatural positioning had been brought about as a result of an altercation with a woman in a Los Angeles bar who turned out to be a man who happened to have a mean right cross. But that was long ago and the only possible witness would have been Paul Haley and he was keeping his mouth shut about those days. Which could well have had something to do with his continued job security.

De Briggi spotted a headline announcing that another business executive had been kidnapped in South America, and he was glad of the comforting presence of Jonas M. Horensen by his side.

Horensen, the Company's chief of security, was a crew-cut all-American boy in his middle fifties, lean, fit and dressed in immaculate grey. He hated commies, niggers and wops, and he didn't think too highly of micks either. At first glance, he might be mistaken for a CIA agent, which was one of several reasons why the CIA had long ago dispensed with his services.

From the ground below, Andrews saw the helicopter begin its partially controlled fall and he called his troops smartly to attention. Then, flanked by O'Shee and Haley, he marched towards the landing area.

The grass was a brilliant green sward set with beads of dancing moisture after the morning rain. But the ground beneath was not as firm as one might have wished for the occasion. Andrews felt his shoes sink into several squelching inches of muck and he made a mental note to chide the planners for failing to provide for such a contingency.

Suddenly he noticed another unplanned item. Around the corner of the plant came a solitary figure, also on course for the descending chopper and there was no mistaking the build and the foliage. It was Horny Harry.

'Oh Christ, no!' Andrews groaned and he lengthened his stride. Harry responded by also stepping up his pace. Andrews and his sidekicks promptly broke into a trot. Not to be outdone, Harry opened up his throttle and hit a canter.

Sergeant O'Meara and Garda O'Shaughnessy were on crowd control duty outside the plant and they were quick to assess the situation.

'Come on, boyo,' the sergeant bawled and they set off at a thundering gallop to intercept Harry.

It was all rather confusing to de Briggi. He could see three men coming in at an easy trot from his left, a lone figure bearing down from the front and two speeding policemen at one o'clock high.

Horensen read the situation at a glance and snapped smoothly into action. In his CIA days, he had been the fastest man on the draw in his section and, even in the confines of the helicopter, he demonstrated no mean ability.

'Subversives!' he yelled and fired two quick warning shots in the air, removing half of the helicopter's perspex dome.

Of the six approaching figures, Andrews was the only one who had been fit enough or dumb enough to have seen military service and he knew exactly how to act under fire.

'Hit the deck!' he shouted and dived full length on the ground. All the others foolishly ignored his advice and ran away.

'Get the friggin' thing up!' yelled de Briggi, and the helicopter withdrew upwards to review the situation from a safer distance.

Andrews lay prone on the ground and, as the clammy

mud came seeping through his clothes and up his nostrils, he began to wonder if he had been guilty of an error of judgement. Slowly, he pulled himself free of the noisily sucking ground and looked down at the slimy mess that covered him from toecaps to eyebrows.

'You stupid goddam son of a bitch,' he roared in the direction of the helicopter.

Then, squelching at every step, he returned to the waiting group and in his eye there was a look that inhibited question or comment. He went directly to his car.

Paul,' he told Haley calmly, 'take over while I go clean up.'

'Sure thing,' Haley assured him.

'If he decides to come down again,' Andrews added, 'tell the goddam – tell him I'll be back shortly.'

The car took Andrews away and Haley surveyed the scene indecisively. At the far side of the green the Sergeant and his help were in full cry after Harry. Nearer home, curious employees were hanging out of windows wondering who had been shot and hoping for a decent view of the corpse.

Haley did not know what the hell to do, so he decided to call a meeting.

'Get those people back to work,' he roared at the wall of the building and the heads withdrew quickly. 'Myles,' he said to O'Shee, 'why don't we go inside and review the position with the MD.'

They went into J. J.'s office to confer.

Up in the deep blue yonder, de Briggi shivered in the icy blast coming through the disintegrating dome and tried to protect his head from the continuing hail of broken perspex.

'You trigger-happy goon,' he shouted at Horensen. 'Where the hell do you think you are? New York?'

'They were coming at us,' Horensen reasoned. 'And besides, nobody was hurt.'

'Someone is gonna be,' de Briggi promised, leaving

143

Horensen in no doubt that he meant Horensen.

The security man made a quick decision. The moment they got back to base, he would defect to Sony or GE or some other competitor where he could be assured of industrial asylum in exchange for the goods he had on some of the Company's senior personnel.

De Briggi, like a famous fellow American, had never been a quitter and moreover he was beginning to feel the first symptoms of exposure.

'Take her down,' he ordered the pilot, 'and if you . . . ' he turned to Horensen, ' . . . as much as lay a pinkie on that goddam gun, I'll ram it up your goddam ass. Butt first.'

Horny Harry had the breed of the fox in him and, while the sergeant and his entire force were combing the streets seeking his scent, he doubled back on his tracks.

And so, as the helicopter came cautiously down again, de Briggi was pleased to note that only one figure was approaching, quite sedately, to greet him. He had never actually met any of his Irish minions, being many organisational layers above them, and for a moment, he was puzzled by the leather jacket and the over-generous hair style. Then he concluded that the American Management, in true colonising spirit, had adapted to their environment.

The great man jumped nimbly from the helicopter. Trying to ignore the fact that his Guccis had gone eyelet-deep in mire, he stretched out his hand cordially, as if greeting an equal.

'Hi there,' he said benevolently.

Horny Harry took hold of the presidential hand and gave it a hearty shake.

'Phook yez,' said he by way of greeting.

De Briggi concluded that he was the recipient of a traditional native greeting.

'And the same to yourself,' he responded.

'An' all belonging-ta-yez,' added Harry.

This one was too much for de Briggi to get his tongue around. He delved in his memory and retrieved another made-in-Hollywood traditional Irish blessing.

'And the top of the morning to yourself,' said he.

'Phookin' Yankie cap'list,' said Harry more distinctly and it was at this point that de Briggi began to feel that all was not well. For the life of him, he could not think of an appropriate reply to that one.

'Doin' a man out of his phookin' Unemployment,' Harry elaborated and then, out of the corner of his eye, he observed the Sergeant coming at him fast.

'Phook the lot of yez,' said he, driving his point home. He gave de Briggi's hand one final hearty shake and withdrew at a gallop, well pleased at the manner in which he had conducted the interview.

And thus the finely tuned schedule that had taken so much sweat and brainwork went smoothly down the spout and the remainder of the programme was played strictly by ear and, consequently, turned out to be quite a success.

Ireland's Taoiseach and no less than two cabinet ministers were present, with millionaire Bill Morgan, softly murmuring in their ears the names of the owners of approaching outstretched hands so that they could be greeted as old friends. It was rumoured, by the begrudgers of course, that Morgan was a major shareholder in leading members of most of the major political parties.

The chairman, vice chairman and sundry members of the County Council, the Urban Council and the Parish Council were there, all in open and hostile competition for proximity to the Taoiseach.

Many other personages were also in attendance, some by invitation, some by infiltration, some by intimidation, all expressing polite wonder and admiration as they were ushered through the more presentable areas of the plant.

At the end of the tour the guests were herded into the canteen for the main event of the day: the bottle opening ceremony and accompanying speeches.

It was a much transformed canteen, with a green-covered table raised on high across one end and, on the table, a daunting array of water jugs and microphones to provide lubrication and amplification for the many speechmakers. On the wall behind the platform, the furled flags of Ireland and the United States were crossed, with the company crest suggestively dangling between them.

As the visitors poured into the canteen, they were drawn irresistibly to the serving counter, now adorned with assorted bottles and glasses and tended by crisp young men in clinical white.

Forewarned by the battery of microphones, the listeners-to-be were quick to avail themselves of the anaesthetic being administered by the crisp young men and they prayed that the supply would not run dry before the speakers did.

The Taoiseach spoke at length of the Company's fine record and at greater length of his party's foresight in bringing such a sophisticated modern industry and so many good jobs to the area.

The chairman of the County Council, who was a member of the opposition, spoke in Irish and English and ringing clichés, endorsing the Taoiseach's praise of the Company. He pointed out delicately however, that, in claiming credit for bringing the factory to Ballyderra, the respected leader was lying in his teeth, because the chairman's own party had been in power at the time. However, he admitted generously, the present crowd had not yet got around to fouling up that particular deal.

Then up rose de Briggi himself and, when Haley had lowered the microphone to catch his every word, he went all choking and emotional about worldwide achievements of his great Company. He followed this up with expressions of great personal pleasure at seeing the beautiful and ancient country of Ireland now benefiting from corporate benevolence. In passing, he gave the Government an indulgent pat on the head for providing such attractive grants and tax holidays to attract foreign industry. Finally he wound up with a stomach-turning eulogy on the intelligence and trainability of the Irish worker.

The following ten speakers, mainly local politicians, repeated themselves and each other with excruciating monotony, each speaker naturally taking the opportunity to score off all opposing parties. To their credit, however, it must be admitted that they showed due regard for the solemnity of the occasion by exercising greater restraint in word and deed than was their custom within their hallowed meeting chambers.

Several verbose hours later, the guests, half blind from flashbulbs and liquor, were ferried to the Lakeside. There they were exposed to some food, more speeches and drinks and the presentation to de Briggi of what purported to be the first Model 660 produced in Ireland, and a good time was had by those strong enough to retain consciousness.

NINETEEN

King could sense that something was seriously amiss.

De Briggi had come and gone. The visiting dignitaries had been right royally wined and dined. But the faithful workers who might have contributed so much to the success of Model 660, if not for the strike, had been cruelly excluded from the celebrations. Small wonder that employee morale, usually so mediocre, was now down at uncarpeted floor level.

'Hey,' King called hoarsely, and Malone opened one poorly focussed eye, 'we'll have to do something about this.'

Malone let the eye fall shut again, but King persisted.

'Look at them,' he nodded towards his colleagues and instantly regretted the movement. 'Their morale is shot to hell.'

'Like my nerves,' Malone groaned. The weekend in Ballybunion had taken its toll, and all he needed was thirty-six hours of complete rest.

As usual, King had been the one who made overtures to the two girls at the disco in Ballybunion. And, as usual, King had ended up with the shapely, sexy one while Malone found himself with the plain, intelligent one with the glasses who wanted nothing but serious conversation. To compensate for the ordeal, he had drunk himself into a stupor. Now he was paying the price.

'Our comrades could do with a motivational injection,' King remarked.

'Up their asses.'

'They deserve a celebration of their own,' King went on,

'and I know just the thing.'

'Please,' begged Malone, 'don't tell me about it.'

On the following day, a notice appeared on the bulletin boards. 'Fellow employees,' it announced, 'our good friend and colleague Ignatius Freely has just got himself engaged. To celebrate the occasion, a party will be held at the Lakeside on Sunday night. The usual collection for the drinking fund will take place. Give generously and come early.'

Almost everyone turned up for the party. At the outset, the investors gave themselves fully to the task of liquidating their assets before someone else did and, for a time, nobody showed any great interest in the whereabouts of the guest of honour.

Then, as the night went steadily downhill, people had some difficulty recalling why they had come in the first place.

The one exception was Mervyn P. Andrews and the more liquid he absorbed the more determined he became to shake the happy couple's respective hands and slap their backs. And so, glass in hand, he meandered about in quest of Ignatius and partner.

It was on one of his frequent detours by the bar that he finally collided with King.

'Hey,' he called, 'you're supposed to be the brain behind this shindig.'

'Who? Me?' King asked modestly.

'Where the hell are they?'

'Who?'

'The happy couple,' Andrews said. 'I want to extend my felic – fel – I want to shake their goddam hands.'

'Oh,' said King whose sharpness of wit was rarely blunted, even by alcohol, ''tis a sad thing entirely.'

'Whaddaya mean?'

King took Andrews by the arm and led him confidentially into a corner.

149

'Promise you won't let it out?' he pleaded.

'Let what out?'

'We don't want to spoil the evening, do we?'

'Of course not,' Andrews agreed, then added impatiently, 'what the hell are you talking about?'

'The engagement is broken off,' King said in a voice choked with sorrow.

'You're kidding!'

'Honest to God,' King assured him. 'Ignatius is just after phoning me. The poor oul' bugger is too embarrassed and upset to show up, and that's understandable, isn't it?'

Andrews nodded in agreement.

'What went wrong?' he asked.

'I don't know for sure,' King said. 'I think their parents fell out over the dowry.'

'You don't say!'

'Happens all the time,' King informed him.

Andrews suddenly discovered that his glass was empty and he laid a course for the bar to re-stock.

Eventually, the money behind the counter came to an end and so did legal Sunday drinking time but Andrews was now so amicably pissed that he committed some of his entertainment budget towards a continuation of the festivities and so the bar re-opened and the hell with the law.

But then, around three-thirty, when the party was just beginning to get into its stride, the company money ran out and so did Andrews and the bar was abruptly shut down.

This event came as an almost sobering shock to the celebrants and, after giving the matter some consideration, they decided they might as well go home, or something.

Malone had drunk himself to the verge of a deep depression. He felt a sudden need for solitude and decided to take himself up to the top of Knockderra Mountain, where he could worry undisturbed.

He went out to the car park and, without too much difficulty, he got his car started and deftly reversed it down the six cement steps into the hotel's ornamental pool.

It so happened that William Alphonsus King was standing on a balcony overlooking the pool at that precise moment and he was quick to react to his friend's dangerous plight. Without a moment's hesitation, he kicked off his shoes.

'Hold on, Jimmy,' he bellowed reassuringly, 'I'm coming,' and, without further ado, he dived from the balcony.

About half way down he remembered that the pool was all of six inches deep but it was now too late to reconsider. He put out his hands and feet to break the impact and this piece of quick thinking almost certainly saved him from serious injury. As it was, his palms and his insteps struck the pebbled bottom of the pool, suffering severe laceration, and whatever wind he had in him at the time left him in one huge gust.

As King lay there belly down in the water, quietly drowning, Malone stepped from his car on to King's upturned anus and from there to the pool's edge, without wetting even a toecap. He then proceeded erratically as far as the town square, where he got into a violent altercation with the statue of Daniel O'Connell.

Garda O'Shaughnessy, who happened to be patrolling in the immediate vicinity, suddenly materialised beside Malone, his little black book at the ready.

'Name?' he demanded forcefully.

'Ignatius Freely,' said Malone.

The Garda got him to spell the name and then told him to go home and sleep it off and to expect a bit of a summons in due course for disturbing the peace.

They went their separate ways, the Garda moving up O'Connell Street towards the barracks and a mug of hot soup, Malone towards King's car, parked in front of the flat.

Back at the hotel, after some deliberation, they decided they might as well drag King from the pool. Into the building they carried him and down the back stairs, bloody but unbowed, to the boiler room where they stripped him to the pelt. They hung his wet clothes to dry over various hot pipes and advised him solicitously not to don a stitch till everything was bone dry or he would end up with double pneumonia. And there they left him, alone and bare.

King found a comfortable spot beside the furnace and went to sleep for himself.

Some hours later, he awoke with the father and mother of a thirst and he realised that if he did not get a drink immediately he would spontaneously combust. He checked his clothes but they were still quite damp and, recalling the warning about double pneumonia, he proceeded in the raw on his quest for a drop of something; anything, as long as it contained a substantial percentage of alcohol.

Up into the lobby he padded and found it dimly lit but deserted. He tried the door to the bar and, to his horror, it was locked.

With growing anxiety, he trotted over to the reception desk and was about to ring the little bell for attention when he heard a car pull up outside.

Through the glass doorway he observed four middle-aged Americans extruding from a taxi. He could tell they were Americans because the two males were topped off with Irish Tartan caps that no self-respecting native would be seen dead in. Laden down with luggage, they came staggering towards the doorway.

Too late, King realised that his line of retreat was cut off. The stairway to his boiler room sanctuary was just inside the front door and, if he now proceeded in that direction, he would certainly come under the scrutiny of the approaching visitors. Instinctively, he felt that the sight of a raw native at that hour might well have an unsettling effect on the newcomers and the possibility that one of them might suffer a heart attack or pull a gun and shoot him down in his prime could not be ruled out.

Quickly, he looked about him in search of a place of

concealment and, back where the light was dim, he spied an alcove in the wall. It had obviously been designed to house a statue but at the moment it was unoccupied. Racking his brain for an appropriate pose, he scuttled towards the niche. In view of his present lack of attire, a Grecian athlete seemed appropriate. He clambered nimbly onto the ledge and assumed an aggressive stance, modestly directing his full frontal to one side.

The guests came nasally vocal into the lobby, bemoaning flight delays and the total ineptitude of every airline that flew the deep blue yonder and wondering how they had been crazy enough ever to leave Springfield, Ohio in the first place.

One of the males confronted the reception desk and began to beat hell out of the inoffensive little bell while the other enquired at a loud bellow whether anyone was at home.

The two ladies, solid in their loose floral dresses and topped off with amazing technicolour hair, prowled the lobby in search of something old to wonder at or something dusty to criticise and it was not long before their gaze fell on the figure in the alcove. They homed in for a closer look and King strove to hold his breath and his balance.

For a while they stood and peered at him in the dim light.

'Graeco-Roman?' one enquired.

'Imitation,' snapped the other, learnedly.

'Probably,' agreed number one. 'Too puny to be the real thing.'

'I got to admit, though,' said number two, 'the detail is real good.'

Their gazes were aimed just below King's navel.

'Yes, indeed,' agreed the one with the mainly pink hair, 'but a bit out of proportion.'

Her companion donned a pair of spectacles, gold-chained to her neck.

'Oh, I don't know, honey,' she said smugly. 'It depends on what you're used to.'

153

'In this light,' Pink Hair remarked, 'it looks almost real.' and she reached out to touch.

'Not on your Nellie!' roared King.

The travellers had had a trying day. Their flight out of Kennedy had been delayed by engine trouble. They had been diverted from Shannon to Dublin because of fog and had waited for several hours for a bus back to Shannon again. And the taxi ride from Shannon, on the wrong side of the road, had sapped most of their remaining stamina.

Now a talking statue, and that was too much!

As one man, they began to scream and, for their ages, they had pretty fair lungs. Frantically, they gathered up their belongings and went through the door at a lively sprint. Their luck was in because the taxi driver was still turning his vehicle on the flower beds outside. Ass-over-elbow, they tumbled into the taxi and never paused till they reached good old predictable New York where there were no talking statues and the worst you could expect was to be knifed in the subway or raped in Central Park, or vice versa.

The hotel night staff were well practiced at ignoring the little bell, but the screams of four hysterical Americans was something else and the manager and the hall porter arrived just in time to witness the escape of the visitors and to capture King on his retreat to the furnace room.

They paused not to ask the why and the wherefore but grabbed King, threw him forcibly into the manager's car and delivered him back to his flat.

They found the key in the mailbox, opened the door and dropped the body disdainfully on the living room floor and then went back to their warm beds.

King lay where he fell, naked as the day he was born, and slept.

Maudie Cahill was one of Ballyderra's most reputable cleaning ladies and was much in demand among those householders who were too busy, delicate or lazy to perform the more menial or physical of their domestic chores. Among her clients she numbered King and Malone, who shared a flat and, as she let herself in to face up to her Monday morning clean-up, the sight that met her weary eyes was daunting, to say the very least.

There on the floor, arms outstretched, in a posture of repose and stark nudity, lay William Alphonsus King.

One of the first things Maudie noticed about the body was its hands, blood-streaked from his dive into the pool. She looked quickly down at his feet, and, behold, they too were bloody.

To a woman as devout as Maudie it could only mean one thing.

Uttering a loud moan of ecstasy, the good woman dropped to her knees beside the body, pulling from her pocket her ever-ready rosary beads. Delicately, she dropped her duster so that it concealed King's gender and then she began to pray with great feeling and volume.

Gradually, King became aware that he was dead. The chill numbness of his extremities, the inability to open an eye or move a muscle, the blankness of his mind, all were clearly identifiable symptoms. But the real clincher was the soft murmur of the Rosary being recited over him. For a while, he lay there at peace and savoured the soothing sound until it lulled him to sleep once more.

When he awoke again the prayer was still flowing over him, perhaps a shade louder, and the whole proceeding would really have been very pleasant were it not for the sensation inside his head. It strongly resembled a lulu of a hangover, but everyone knew that corpses couldn't suffer from such a malady. He concluded that it must be jet lag.

Then, suddenly, his serenity was disturbed by a discordant male voice.

'What the bloody hell is going on?' it demanded.

155

Maudie shushed the interrupter gently, and went on with her frenzied prayers.

But Malone, returning with a hangover all his very own, and after several hours of cramped sleep in King's car half way up Knockderra Mountain was in no mood to be shushed.

'King, you gobshite, you!' he shouted and one of the corpse's eyes sprang open of its own accord.

To King's surprise, the eye could see. Not very clearly, and tinged with red, but vision there indisputably was. The other eye opened for corroboration, and corroboration there also was.

Malone poked a cold toecap under King's rump and pushed and it was at about this time that King began to revise his original diagnosis. He felt the hard shoe dig into his rear and the nausea in his stomach and the hammering inside his head and he concluded that he was not dead after all, though he began devoutly to wish that he was.

'Shag off,' he told Malone hoarsely and he rolled over, dislodging the duster. Without missing a single syllable of her Hail Mary, Maudie dropped it back on target again.

Malone turned to the good woman, puzzled.

'What are you doing?' he enquired.

Maudie bobbed her head vigorously at the word 'Jesus' and kept on going.

'Will you answer me,' Malone demanded and Maudie pointed reverently in King's direction, still without a break in her prayerful flow.

Malone bent and caught her by the arms and shook her.

'Is it out of your mind you are!' he shouted, and finally he had her attention.

'Look at his hands!' she whispered. 'Look at his feet!'

'What are you talking about?'

'The stigmata! The marks of the nails!' and she was away in another burst of prayer.

It took a strong physical effort but Malone eventually

got her though the door, still praying and raising her volume as she was moved farther away from the object of her devotion.

Then he turned to scowl down at King.

'What was that all about?' King croaked.

'Don't ask me.'

'Jesus,' said King, 'I'm dying.'

'How do you think I feel?' Malone complained, 'I spent the night in your bloody car up the bloody mountain.'

Very slowly and unsteadily, King struggled to his knees and crawled to the bathroom to put his head under the cold tap. There was a long silence except for their continuous groans and curses and Maudie's prayers wafting in through the door.

'Oh God!' exclaimed Malone. 'What time is it at all?'

King didn't bother to reply, and Malone finally got his eyes to focus.

''Tis after ten!' he announced in dismay.

'Who cares?' King wanted to know.

'We're dead late for work.'

'I'm not late,' King corrected him. 'I'm absent.'

'Did you phone in?' Malone asked.

'How could I phone in and I unconscious?'

'I'd better do it.' Malone went out to the phone in the hallway, past the entranced figure of Maudie.

'What'll I tell them?' he shouted to King.

'Who cares?' King repeated as he came out of the bathroom, towelling himself tenderly.

Malone telephoned Haley and informed him that King was delirious after last night's debauchery and was likely to jump out of the window if left alone.

Haley tried to encourage Malone to come to work, hoping that King would then jump and break his goddam neck but he finally compromised when Malone undertook to check in as soon as the doctor arrived and gave King a sedative.

'You lying bastard,' said King, throwing the towel at Malone.

In the passageway outside, Maudie picked the towel up to tidy it away. Then she noticed the bloodstains. Never in her life had the decent woman taken anything that did not belong to her but this was temptation beyond her powers of resistance. From that day, the towel hung reverently on her kitchen wall, bloodstains and all, between John F. Kennedy and the Sacred Heart.

TWENTY

It was another deceitfully lovely late Autumn morning; the world glittering in the clear, bright sunshine, a few innocent-looking, fluffy clouds hanging around, a hint of chill in the air. And, though Collins didn't realise it as he walked along the Cosaun to the plant, it was the start of one of the most portentous days of his working life.

Cosán na Naomh, the path of the saints, ribboned down behind him to the old Abbey in the valley while, ahead of him, it meandered all the way up Knockderra as far as *Carraig na bPaidir,* the saddle-shaped rock at the summit.

The Abbey was founded by St Malachy, who had defected from St Brendan's crowd in Kerry because of a difference of opinion about taking off on strange voyages. The only voyage that counted, according to Malachy, was the one from here to eternity and he had little time for Brendan's gallivanting off to the west in his canvas boat where he was bound to fall over the edge of the world and end up in hell.

Tradition had it that the Cosaun had been worn into the hillside by the pious feet of Malachy and his followers on their frequent penitential trips between the Abbey and *Carraig na bPaidir,* the Rock of the Prayers.

Tradition also had it that Malachy, not to be outdone by anyone, however exalted, had sat on *Carraig na bPaidir* and fasted for forty-one days and forty-one nights and had then been carried triumphantly back down to the Abbey where he expired from malnutrition and exposure,

159

and in an overpowering odour of sanctity.

On its uphill way from the Abbey to the rock, the Cosaun was intersected, first by the main Limerick to Kerry road, then by Parnell Street, then by the river at its shallowest point, where the holy monks had waded across long before bridges were invented. It finally took leave of the town just beyond the laneways of Irishtown and continued on its way up the mountain in a series of zigs and zags. Four zigs to the west and five zags to the east.

Collins came to the junction where the Cosaun cut across Parnell Street. The Friary bell started to ring for half-eight mass. Seven or eight people on the street, mostly women, on their way to mass.

A lone car – *Cork registration* – came, too fast along the narrow street.

He saw his mother come out the front door beside the shop, dark-clothed, behatted, a large missal under her right arm.

'Hello Mam,' he called.

'Brianeen,' she greeted him querulously, 'you never come to see me any more.'

'Wasn't I up last Tuesday!'

'Just a hello and goodbye,' she said sarcastically. 'And you know I haven't been feeling too well.'

– *The healthiest hypochondriac in Ballyderra* –

'You'll have to come over this evening, now.'

– *Humour her* –

'Right you are, Mam.'

'And bring Lucy. How is she?'

'Oh, fine. Fine.'

'Without fail, now, mind.' She shifted the load of her missal from left arm to right. 'I'll be late for Mass.' And off with her at her usual busy trot, her thin body tilted sharply forward like an athlete straining for the finishing tape.

Collins looked after her and smiled.

– The Ma . . . still fasts from midnight thinks it's still a sin to eat meat on Fridays and misses the mystique of the Latin Mass –

– DON'T MOCK YOUR MOTHER! –

–I did no such thing! –

– AFTER ALL SHE HAD TO PUT UP WITH –

– His funeral came up along the street . . . stopped for a full two minutes in front of the shop and the blinds pulled down on all the windows along the street and people blessing themselves when we passed . . . the new one-way street put an end to all that now it's the shortest way from the church to the graveyard and get it over with . . . sad.

Charlie the postman came out of the post office, with his bag over his shoulder.

'Brian,' Charlie called, 'I have a couple for you.' He reached into his bag and produced four letters.

'Sound man, yourself.' Collins glanced at his mail. The telephone bill, a bill from the hospital for Lucy's tests, – *Everyone has their bloody hands out* – a maternity wear catalogue, – *probably ordered by her mother* – and the letter from Leading Edge.

– Oh Jesus this is it –

Charlie looked up at the sky.

'You're going to be wet by the time you get to work,' he said as he produced his waterproof cape and wrapped it around his shoulders.

Collins saw the grey glisten of the shower as it came at him around the mountain. He stuck the letters in his pocket and started to run along the boreen.

– Shit shit shit – And it wasn't the weather that was bothering the little voice.

Collins was not in the mood for meditation this morning. The letter lay there on his otherwise clear desk, unopened. It reflected a pale light from the morning sun. Balefully. And, as Charlie had prophesied, he was soaking wet.

– Open the bloody thing –

He removed his jacket, a darker grey now from the rain, and hung it on the steel hanger behind the door.

– Will you open it –

He stabbed the envelope viciously with his letter-opener, a delicate, sword-shaped souvenir from Spain.

The now-familiar letter heading. The now-familiar signature, and, in between the two:

Dear Brian

As a result of the top-level meetings that have detained me for so long at Headquarters, our Corporation has reached a number of highly significant and far-reaching decisions which will have a major impact on our product lines, our business strategies and our overall organisational structure.

– What's this bullshit? –

Regretfully, as a consequence of these decisions, we will not be going ahead with our proposed Irish subsidiary in the foreseeable future.

– Jesus be praised and that's not swearing –

I know this will come as a great disappointment to you.

– Like hell it does! –

Collins began to laugh aloud with delight.

But it may be some consolation to you that you were definitely our candidate of choice for the position. I would have really enjoyed having you on our management team. Perhaps our paths may cross again in the future. Meanwhile, let me offer you my best wishes for your future success.

– You're off the hook boy! –

He folded the letter and put it carefully back in its envelope.

As a penance for taking such pleasure from an event that

would certainly shatter Lucy, he got up and took the letter to his boss's office.

Andrews's smile was at its broadest as he strode into Jennifer Carey's presence. He dropped the handwritten Personnel Change Form on his boss's table and she glanced briefly at it. Brian Collins's name at the top and all those approval signatures at the bottom.

'We can tear it up, J. J.,' Andrews announced. 'He hasn't got the job.'

'You're sure?' J. J. asked.

'He just showed me the letter. They're abandoning the Irish operation.'

J. J. looked thoughtfully at the high-powered signatures on the form again.

'Did Collins know,' she asked, 'that you were processing this increase for him?'

Andrews hesitated, then decided that it was better to tell the truth than to be found out later.

'Not in so many words,' he confessed, 'but I dropped a couple of broad hints. Just to make sure he wouldn't make any hasty decisions.'

J. J. was obviously puzzled.

'Why didn't he hold out to see what might develop?'

'Dumb.'

'Or honest?'

'Same thing.'

But J. J. was considering the possibility that there might actually be an honest man in her organisation.

'He didn't try to grab the credit for fixing the strike either,' she said thoughtfully.

'Anyhow we can tear that up.' Andrews pointed to the form.

J. J. nodded. Slowly, deliberately, she began to tear all five copies down the middle, then several times across from side to side.

163

There was a silence for a moment. Then J. J. nodded emphatically to herself.

'Take a seat, Merv,' she said cordially as she buzzed her secretary on the intercom.

'Agnes,' she said, 'would you mind getting Brian Collins in here right away.'

Andrews's smile drifted north into his nostrils.

'Now, Merv,' J. J. leaned earnestly across the black-top table, 'here's what we're going to do. We're going to promote Brian to the position of Associate Director of Human Resources.'

'There's no such position!'

'There is now!'

'But J. J. – '

'And', J. J. went on inexorably, 'we're going to give him a fifteen per cent pay increase, make him eligible for a company car and move him into that empty three-window office beside yours. And when you transfer back to the mainland he'll move into your slot here.'

All this was too much for Andrews's smile.

'J. J.,' he stammered, 'there's no way we can . . .'

J. J. was now the only one smiling. Andrews thought she had a lovely smile, teeth white and even, but he wished he hadn't detected the hint of malevolent glee behind it.

'You'd like to get back to the mainland reasonably soon, wouldn't you?'

Andrews nodded quickly and J. J. leaned back, knowing well that she had just pressed Andrews's most powerful motivational button.

'I want to make damn sure,' she went on, 'we don't lose Brian to some other headhunter.'

'But J. J.,' said Andrews earnestly, 'we'll never get approval for this.'

'I think,' J. J. reassured him, 'I can help in that area. Just let me have a bundle of Personnel Change notices and I'll take care of the paperwork. OK?'

'Who'll sign off on it?' Andrews asked nervously.

'I will.'

You gutless wonder, she thought to herself.

Andrews's smile almost returned. When the shit hit the fan on this wild idea, he could claim innocence.

Collins appeared in the doorway, looking a trifle uneasy.

'Brian,' J. J. got straight to the point. 'I understand from Merv that the job offer from that bunch in Dublin didn't materialise.'

'That's right.'

'Were you aware that Merv was putting together a counter-offer – a salary increase – for you?'

'Well, I had a suspicion.'

'Then why did you tell Merv you were turned down?'

– *Put her right on that* –

'I wasn't exactly turned down. They're simply not going ahead with the project.'

J. J. nodded.

'I understand,' she said, 'I understand. But you knew there was a salary increase in the pipeline. Why didn't you hold off to see what might come out of it?'

– *Integrity!* –

'I wouldn't want to get anything under false pretences, Miz Carey.'

'Hell, call me J. J.' She pointed to the chair beside Andrews. 'Take a seat, Brian. Merv and I have some good news for you.'

Collins sat benumbed and bewildered as J. J. laid the good news on him. Even the two inner voices were struck dumb.

He realised that J. J. had just asked a question.

'I presume that's OK with you, Brian?'

Collins could only nod.

'Anything you'd like me to clarify?'

Collins could only shake his head.

'OK,' said J. J., 'I guess you need some time to get

used to the idea.'

– The understatement of the year –

'Merv,' J. J. went on, 'why don't you draft an announcement, making the promotion effective immediately.'

'Who'll sign it?'

'I will, goddam it.'

Andrews nodded. His ass was at least partially covered.

Over the following thirty minutes two urgent telephone calls were made to headquarters.

Andrews bleated the whole story to the Vice-President of Human Resources, warning him of the impossible proposals about to be put forward by J. J. and disclaiming all responsibility.

Meanwhile, J. J. was in briefer conversation with de Briggi.

'Mr de Briggi,' she was saying, 'just calling to confirm that I'll be happy to accept the job offer of Vice-President, West Europe.'

'Good,' said de Briggi, 'I'm glad to hear it.'

'There's just one thing,' J. J. went on. 'If I'm to give it my best shot, I'll need to make some organisational changes.'

'You got it,' de Briggi assured her.

'Some of the changes I have in mind might not go down too well with Personnel.'

'So what's new?'

'I can count on your support?'

'Any shithead that objects better order his coffin.'

'Thank you, Mr de Briggi.'

'Hell, J. J., call me Phil.'

J. J. hung up and went into a serious one-woman conclave.

TWENTY-ONE

At times like this, when important decisions had to be made, Jennifer J. Carey liked to talk the situation through with a trusted subordinate. Not that she really needed anyone else's opinion, but the act of voicing her thoughts helped her to get everything clear in her own mind. Soon after she arrived at the Irish operation she took stock of trustworthy subordinates and the total came to plus or minus zero. She was well aware of the fact that they resented being put in a subordinate position to a woman. Moreover she was quick to realise that any secrets she might reveal to them would not only pander to their chauvinism but would promptly be passed along, with judicious distortions, to their respective political allies in Philadelphia. There, everything would be carefully taken down and used as evidence or weaponry against her at the appropriate time. Given the devious thoughts that were now running through her mind she felt the need more than ever for a discreet listener.

'Collins,' she thought, 'I wonder . . .'

– *A three-window office and a bigger desk . . . finally rid of that bloody picture . . . and a Company car . . . get that photo of Lucy enlarged and framed for the desk and your diplomas on the wall the photo of the College Rugby team the year you played* –

– OH, COME OFF IT –

– *Well maybe just the diploma and the photo of Lucy . . . the new model Renault or an Audi . . . the Audi I think nice lines anything but a Ford –*

– Oh-oh –

Jennifer Carey was standing in the open doorway. 'You busy, Brian?' she enquired.

Without waiting for an answer, she came in, pointedly closing the door. She came over and perched herself on the corner of the desk.

– *Damn nice legs* –

It felt good to be on the receiving end of admiring glances from handsome young men but it was a luxury that she had learned to deny herself. She unhitched herself from the desk and pulled up a chair.

'We need to have a confidential chat, Brian.'

– *You hear that* –

The little voice was impressed with Collins's new status. 'Sure, Miz Carey,' he said.

'Hell,' she smiled, 'you got to get used to calling me J. J.'

'Right.' But such familiarity, especially with a lady boss, didn't come easy to Collins.

'I like that picture,' J. J. remarked as she sat.

– *Why argue* –

'Not bad,' said Collins.

'Now.' J. J. leaned towards Collins. The body language was clear. Just between the two of us, it said. 'What I'm about to tell you is strictly confidential. OK?'

'Absolutely.' Collins nodded, reinforcing the word with emphatic body language of his own.

'Not to be discussed with anyone,' J. J. went on. 'Not even with Merv.'

Collins nodded again.

'*Especially* not with Merv,' J. J. emphasised.

Another vehement nod from Collins.

'First,' J. J. said, 'let me put things in context. Our Company has just taken over an electronics manufacturing operation in Spain, which will report to me along with the Irish operation. My new title will be Vice-President, West

Europe Operations.'

Collins jumped to his feet and shook hands heartily with the new Vice-President.

'Congratulations!' His pleasure was obvious. 'Congratulations, ah, J. J.'

J. J. found the sincerity most refreshing. Her other minions would have used the same words but they would have rung hollow and envious or patronisingly masculine.

'Now,' she went on, 'I intend to make you responsible for the Human Resources functions in both countries.'

– *Jesus, Mary and Holy St Joseph!* –

Collins's voices then went dead as they always did in times of excitement or stress.

'Your title will be Director of Human Resources, West Europe,' J. J. went on, savouring Collins's reaction. 'Reporting to me.'

– *Oh God! this is too much!* –

'What about Merv?' Collins managed to ask.

'Merv's assignment here is nearly up.' J. J.'s smile showed a certain amount of anticipation. 'He'll be moving back to the States.' The smile broadened a little. 'Sooner, rather than later.'

– *Director, West Europe* –

– PRIDE GOETH BEFORE A FALL –

– *Oh shut up you* –

'That's one of the reasons I don't want to go public on all this for the moment,' J. J. explained. 'I want to wait until Merv's transfer comes through.'

Once again, Collins could only nod.

'Meanwhile, I want you to put some wheels in motion,' J. J. told him. 'Quietly. The Spanish Personnel function is still in the Dark Ages. You'll have to hire someone over there and train them. Also, you'll need to get a number two guy in here pretty fast. Can you get a headhunter to start a discreet search?'

'How would you feel . . . ' Collins was now firing on all

169

cylinders and thinking much faster than normal. ' . . . about appointing someone from inside the organisation.'

'Christ!' said J. J., 'not from Headquarters! No way!'

'No,' Collins assured her. 'I was thinking of someone from here.'

'There's no one around here with Personnel experience.'

'I had no Personnel experience when I joined. And, to tell you the truth, I found it harder to learn about the organisation than about Personnel work.'

J. J. thought about that for a moment, then she nodded in understanding.

'Got anyone in mind?' she asked.

'Well . . . Someone like Willie King, maybe.'

J. J. shook her head impatiently.

'No way!' she snapped. 'Not King.'

— *Oh-Oh, Willie's in the shit for something* —

'OK,' J. J. said, 'think about it. See if you can come up with any other names.'

'Oh, another thing,' she added. 'You'd better organise a crash course in Spanish for yourself.'

Collins shook his head and J. J. misunderstood the gesture.

'Hey, you'll need some kind of handle on the language. You'll be spending time over there.'

'Actually,' Collins said, 'I speak Spanish fluently.'

'You don't say!' J. J. was impressed.

'I took honours Spanish for my degree and I taught it for six years.'

'Jesus,' said J. J., 'do I know how to pick 'em!'

TWENTY-TWO

Lucy looked up, startled, as he came into the kitchen. She was wearing her bright yellow apron, her hair was slightly dishevelled. Her bulge was showing a bit more, but very attractively. She had the blender going, which explained why she hadn't heard the gate's welcoming squeal.

– *God, she's beautiful* –

'You're early,' she said accusingly.

'That's some welcome.'

She laughed and came over to hug him. As she did, she sensed his tension. Bad news. She checked out his expression. What he believed was his poker face, but the eyes always betrayed him. Excited or angry or disappointed. The job in Dublin.

'What brought you home so early?' she asked brightly.

'It's half past five.'

'You never get home before six.'

'You're not complaining, are you?'

'Of course not, sweetheart.' Whatever bad news he had, she was going to make light of it for his sake.

She began to spoon paté into the little individual tubs they had bought in Toledo three years ago.

He leaned casually against the door.

'Right,' he said, 'which do you want first? The good news or the bad news?'

'You decide.' But a small morsel of paté fell on the floor and she didn't even bother to pick it up.

Collins put an arm around her expanded waist.

171

'Maybe you ought to sit down for this.'

She didn't really want to sit but she allowed him to lead her to the seat by the table. She looked anxiously up at him.

'It's the job in Dublin, isn't it?'

Collins nodded.

'It's not on, I'm afraid.'

Lucy got quickly to her feet again and put her arms comfortingly around him.

'Oh, Brian. I'm so sorry. You must be terribly disappointed.'

– *Disappointed? That's all she knows –*

'Ah, you know I wasn't all that keen on moving anyway.'

'That's not what I mean. I know how much you hate to lose. You're such a competitor.'

– *Killer –*

'Actually,' Collins took the letter from his pocket, 'it wasn't exactly like that.'

Lucy read the letter quickly.

'"The candidate of choice",' she quoted, smiling.

'That's me.'

'That's all right, then. I knew all along you were the one they'd pick.'

– *Jesus isn't she full of surprises –*

'I'm sorry, sweetheart,' he said. 'I know how much you were looking forward to a move to Dublin.'

'No. No. I'm not the least put out over that,' she assured him and was surprised to realise that she really meant it. If he had got the job offer they would have had to make a no-win decision. Because if Brian agreed to the move it would have been on her account and if she had opted to stay in Ballyderra, which she very well might have, it would have been on Brian's account. Either way, one or both of them would have had to carry a load of guilt.

'Anyway,' she laughed, 'there will be other chances.'

– *God forbid! –*

172

She took a can of Harp from the fridge and tossed it to him.

'So let's celebrate,' she told him and, as he opened the can she held out two glasses.

'Just a teeny drop for me,' she told him. She was off alcohol for the duration of her pregnancy. 'But before we celebrate the good news, tell me the bad news?'

'Well,' Collins said seriously, 'after I showed that letter to Merv I was called up to J. J.'s office.'

'And she tells me I'm no longer Personnel and Training Manager.'

'Jesus, Mary and Joseph! They didn't fire you, Brian!'

'No, ma'am. You're looking at the new Associate Director of Human Resources. So show a little respect.'

'They promoted you?'

'Fifteen per cent salary increase. Effective immediately.'

'Brian!'

'Company car. Stock options. Executive bonus scheme. Three-window office. And, lady, that ain't all!'

He went on to tell her about the promised promotion to Director of Human Resources for West Europe.

Lucy listened with growing incredulity and delight.

Collins finished his narrative with a word of warning.

'All this,' he cautioned her, 'is top secret until J. J. puts out an official announcement.'

'Surely,' she protested, 'I can tell Mammy and Daddy.'

'Well, I don't-'

– She'll tell them anyway –

'All right. As long as you swear them to secrecy.'

Lucy sat and tried to compose herself.

'Is the candidate of choice going to get fed tonight?' Collins asked.

'My candidate of choice,' Lucy kissed him, 'can have anything he wants.'

– Jesus I think she means it! –

And she did. Up to a point.

TWENTY-THREE

As he sat behind his cigar, presiding over his Department meeting, Haley was in benevolent mood and with good reason. Autumn was blending into a gentle winter. The clocks had gone back an hour and the Model 660 workers were all fully trained, and the first batch of radios were assembled, packed and ready for a mass assault on the British market. Haley was quietly confident that he was a candidate for the Company's Top Management Award, a distinction which, to date, had successfully eluded him.

He even went a little easier on O'Keeffe on the problem of the warping circuit boards, still unsolved, but now on the back burner because the old Model K radio had been pushed out of the limelight by the potentially more profitable 660.

The meeting was in its final spasms when Jennifer J. Carey joined the little group. It would have been difficult to tell that she was angry but for the faint blush on her cheek and the fact that she came in screaming at the top of her voice.

'Who the Christ,' she yelled, waving a fax, 'ordered that million 660 kits from Hong Kong?'

Haley sensed that all was not well.

'Purchasing,' said he smartly.

'Who,' demanded J. J., 'was the shithead who dreamed up the goddam project?' She didn't bother to wait for a reply. 'And who was the birdbrain,' she continued, 'that figured we would make ten million dollars profit on the British market?'

Like George Washington, Haley could not tell a lie with all the evidence stacked against him. On the other hand, neither was he about to be trapped into a direct admission.

'Hell, J.J.,' he said, 'there's nothing on the market to compete with them.'

'You don't say!' shouted J. J., and she pushed the fax towards Haley as if she was about to ram it down the unfortunate man's throat. 'And supposing I told you those two-timing crooks from Orient Electronics have just flooded the British market with identical radios.'

Haley was taken aback, but not for long.

'Aw, we can compete,' he said confidently. 'Don't forget that extra discount.'

J. J. began to jump up and down.

'Compete, my ass,' she shrilled. 'They're selling in the friggin' stores for less than we paid for the friggin' kits, even allowing for your friggin' discount.'

Haley felt the spit dry up in his mouth and it was an old, familiar sensation that told him someone might be due to go off the high diving board.

'Jumping Jesus,' J. J. was now warming to her subject. 'And we've already got five thousand completed sets in the stores.'

Haley knew the figure was actually ten thousand but this was not the time to nitpick.

'I'm holding a meeting in my office in fifteen minutes,' J. J. announced. 'Be there!'

Haley nodded.

'As of right now,' J. J. added, 'all production on the Model 660 is stopped. All efforts are to be directed back to the Model K, while we evaluate the situation.'

J. J. marched out and they could hear her repeating her performance for the benefit of the Purchasing Department at the far end of the building.

Haley's meeting was never formally adjourned but his subordinates faded discreetly away as their master buried

175

one haggard face in two trembling hands.

Outside, King chuckled mischievously.

'Blood will flow,' he announced, 'and heads will roll.'

'Christ,' thought O'Keeffe, 'that puts the pressure back on the warping PCBs,' and his heart grew heavy.

'I wonder,' asked Malone, always the worrier, 'if it'll mean a lay-off?'

Back in her office once more, J. J. was considering ways and means of breaking the bad news to her boss, Fred Williams, while still managing to survive the outcome. She knew she had just one thing going for her. Survival in the corporate war-zone depended on looking good in the eyes of the all-powerful ones, or at least not looking bad. Achievements were all very well, but they carried far less weight than appearances. And when a subordinate landed in the manure, some of the smelly stuff always splashed upwards and tarnished the image of his or her leader.

So, while Fred Williams would undoubtedly heap abuse on his subordinate's innocent head, they had a common interest in minimising the damage to their respective careers.

On the desk in front of J. J. was an oversized scribbling pad. Across the top of the pad she had written in large, blood-red capitals:

PROBLEM = OPPORTUNITY

Beneath the heading, the paper was covered with a jumbled assortment of numbers, key words, doodles. All enclosed in individual boxes, in a variety of colours and connected to each other in a complex mind-map of the problem – correction – opportunity.

She navigated her way one more time through the thought-pattern diagrams; then, with some reluctance, picked up the telephone and dialled Fred Williams's private number.

'Fred,' she asked, 'is your door closed?'

Williams got the message and J. J. waited while he went and closed his door.

'Yeah?' Williams asked. He had picked up the negative vibes and his tone was not cordial.

'I've got a problem and an opportunity,' J. J. told him.

'OK.' For Williams the vibes were confirmed. 'Lay the problem on me first.'

J. J. laid the problem on the man and then waited for several painful minutes until the long-distance hysteria began to abate.

'Can I tell you about opportunities?' she finally asked.

'They better be real good!'

J. J. talked fast and forcefully to preclude any interruptions before she could get the whole thing off her chest.

'Fred,' she said, 'a few years back I was given a development assignment with Marketing. And one of the jobs I did was an analysis of promotional gifts. You know the kind of thing. They give briefcases, clocks, desk-sets, things like that to good customers. With the Company logo on them as a reminder. Well, my analysis showed that the average cost of these gifts was twenty dollars and Marketing's annual budget for this stuff, worldwide was one point six million dollars.'

She heard a guttural sound on the line.

'Wait. Let me finish,' she said quickly. 'Suppose Marketing decided to give our customers gifts of miniature radios for the next couple of years. We could charge them fifteen dollars apiece. That would give them a budget saving of twenty-five percent. They'd be looking good.'

'I'm listening.'

'After all, they owe us big for covering their asses on the oversupply of Model K radios. And, at fifteen dollars apiece,

177

we'd make the same profit as we were expecting from the UK Market.'

'Yeah,' said Williams thoughtfully.

'You think you could swing it?'

'I got a couple of clubs I can use on the sons of bitches,' Williams said. 'Yeah. I think I can swing it.'

'Another thing, Fred,' J. J. felt she was on a roll. 'You know the gifts that Personnel give out to employees around the world? You know, five-year, ten-year anniversaries, special achievements and so on.'

'Yeah,' Williams had caught on.

'They must give out thousands every year.'

'Yeah,' said Williams again, 'most of those things cost over fifteen bucks. We could offer *them* a cost saving too. Provided they take at least two-years supply.'

'Right on.'

'Good thinking, J. J.' Williams was beginning to sound almost happy at the prospect of screwing his friends in Marketing and Personnel, 'I'll get to work on it right away.'

On this positive note they hung up.

J. J. decided to keep her head down and make no announcements about lay-offs until Williams reported back on his negotiations with Marketing and Personnel.

Meanwhile, the Company's lawyers went happily to work, preparing legal proceedings against those perfidious Oriental rogues for breach of agreement or something, which was of little consolation to anyone except the lawyers, who knew they were on a winner no matter how the case went.

After a brief nervous breakdown, O'Shee began to realign his production groups. People who had once been experts on the old Model K, and who had been retrained for the 660, were now being retrained back again for the Model K. The small mountain of old reject Model K chassis was taken out of hiding at the back of the stores and the granny shift was put to work cannibalising parts to repair the more salvageable units. Some were assigned to house-keeping and decorating jobs and longer breaks were allotted to nature's calls.

Andrews took to studying the Redundancy Payments Act, trying, not too successfully, to figure out how much a redundancy would cost and how much could be recovered from the Government's benevolence.

Collins sat in his new three-window office.

– *Big teak desk well teak laminate . . . blue-grey carpet goodbye cold tiles . . . teak-topped credenza OK, laminate . . . framed photo of Lucy beside the telephone looking terrific in that pink blouse let them eat their hearts out! IMI and IPM certificates on the wall nothing ostentatious . . . large black and white of the University Rugby team yourself third from the right at the back –*

– NOTHING OSTENTATIOUS! –

– *Goodbye to the awful seascape and now you have your own confessional corner with a glass-topped table –*

But the shine of the promotion and the new surroundings was greatly dimmed by the sense of impending calamity. J. J. had confided the whole problem-opportunity situation to him and it was clear to both of them that, even if Williams succeeded in making his deals at Headquarters, there would have to be some lay-offs. Such a catastrophe had never before struck Ballyderra and its consequences would be felt far and wide.

He had already spent unhappy hours drawing up a last-in-first-out list. Many of the names near the top were people he knew well. People whose dignity and pride would be severely bruised. People whose families would feel the pinch.

Horny Harry came strolling into the office with Liz Connors valiantly but vainly trying to impede his progress.

'Will I call Security?' Liz asked.

'Jawsus,' Harry assured her, 'I amn't goin' to ate him.'

Collins knew that whatever Harry had in mind would be accomplished by the time Security got there anyway.

''Tis all right, Liz,' he assured her courageously and she went out, leaving the door slightly ajar so that she could hear any cries of distress from her master.

Harry cast a malice-moistened eye over the new office. 'Jawsus,' said he, 'comin' up in the world, aren't we, now?' He took a look out of the middle window. 'And the oul' pinto pony waitin' outside for you to ride off into the sunset.'

He was referring to the new Ford Estate, black and red, in Collins's personalised parking space outside.

– *You really wanted an Audi* –

– LUCY WAS RIGHT. THE ESTATE WILL BE MORE PRACTICAL FOR THINGS LIKE PRAMS AND CARRYCOTS –

Harry sat, uninvited, across the desk from him.

'What do you want, Harry?' Collins asked, with an obvious show of resignation.

'Comereta me,' said Harry pleasantly, 'wasn't the oul' Union on about takin' yez to the Labour Court?'

'What if they were?'

'What are you going to do about it?'

'The case will be thrown out by the court.'

– *You hope* –

'It might and it mightn't,' Harry got up and closed the door carefully and Liz immediately called Security.

'Comereta me,' he said, 'I can give you a way out.'

'I know,' Collins responded sarcastically, 'take you back without loss of pay.'

'I'd be willing to drop the loss of pay bit,' Harry said. 'Just take me back an' fire me.'

– *Watch out* –

'Nothing doing.' Collins shook his head emphatically.

'Sure all I want,' said Harry earnestly, 'is to get fired so that I can draw my unemployment.'

Collins shook his head again.

'Sure what odds?' Harry argued. 'Aren't ye going to shut down the phookin' joint anyway?'

'No we're not,' Collins insisted, and then the idea struck him with force.

– *The redundancy list* –

'Supposing,' he asked quickly, 'we took you back and then made you redundant, would you go away and leave us in peace?'

'Would that get me my unemployment?'

'It'd get you redundancy money and that's at least as good.'

– FALSIFYING RECORDS. YOU CAN'T –

'You're on!' said Harry happily.

'And you'd drop the Labour Court case?'

'From a height,' Harry assured him, 'and the phookin' oul' Union along with it.'

– Defrauding the government –

– *Doesn't everyone* –

The temptation was too great.

'You'll have to bring in your social welfare card,' he said.

Harry reached in his hip pocket, and slapped the card, oily and much creased, smartly down on the desk.

Within three minutes and without undue pomp and circumstance, Horny Harry was reinstated, made redundant and sent on his merry way.

No sooner was Harry safely off the premises than an ageing but far from stupid security guard arrived to offer asthmatic assistance.

TWENTY-FOUR

Jennifer J. Carey was a direct kind of person who preferred everything out in the open, and the ordeal of keeping her head down and her mouth shut during those difficult days was not at all to her liking. But eight days had passed and still Williams had not concluded negotiations with Marketing and Personnel.

The trouble with official silence in times of uncertainty is that the credibility gap is filled with unofficial rumours which radiate in ever-increasing circles of ever-increasing inaccuracy. And rumours of the impending doom of Worldwide Electronics followed this precise pattern, till the entire countryside from the Feale River to the lordly Shannon, had it on reliable but unidentifiable authority that the company had gone bankrupt and was about to go into liquidation.

When this abominable rumour finally came to J. J.'s ears, she rose to it like a trout in the Owenderra river to the offal from the town abbatoir. Here, at least, was something she could sink her teeth into. Here was an opportunity for positive action; time for a solemn and public declaration of faith.

J. J. placed the draft memo on Collins's desk. 'I'd like your opinion on this, Brian?'

Collins read the memo, which was written in confident capitals:

It has come to my attention that a malicious
rumour is currently in circulation: our Company
is said to be about to close down. Each and every
one of you has my personal assurance that there
is no truth in this false and scandalous story.

> Signed J. J. Carey
> Managing Director

'What do you think?' J. J. asked, impatient to go into action.
'I think it might cause problems,' Collins told her cautiously.
'What kind of problems, for Chrissake?'

'It's just a gut feeling,' Collins said apologetically.
'Can you give me a little time to think it through?'

'Aw, shit!' said J. J. and she took the note with her
to Andrews's office, seeking a supporting opinion from
someone who had grown up with the corporate philosophy:
When there's a problem, you gotta be seen to do something.
Also known as the activity syndrome.

Andrews was quick to discern the answer his boss wanted
to hear.

'Looks great to me, J. J.,' he pronounced.

Twenty minutes later the memo appeared on all company
bulletin boards and, within an hour, copies had been pressed
into the hands of all employees who happened to be at their
workplaces.

And thus, with one masterly and unintentional stroke of
genius, J. J. solved the redundancy problem, because
there is no better way on this earth of reinforcing a
rumour than by coming out in public and insisting that
it's not true. And the more emphatic the denial the more
the rumour is reinforced.

Those who had not yet heard of the Company's dire

straits wondered why such an announcement was called for and they promptly concluded that it was a smokescreen to hide the fact that the Company was, in fact, about to fold its tent. On the other hand, those who had heard the rumour already found their worst fears confirmed when they saw it there in black and white on the notice boards.

And so, by the following Monday morning, a large proportion of the more mobile and more employable employees had deserted the sinking ship and had been offered gainful employment in the industrial estates in Limerick and Shannon, and Collins had gratefully fed his redundancy lists to the shredder lest the remaining faithful might discover how many of their number had been destined for the high jump.

In order to maintain some semblance of normality about the place, J. J. demanded to see the most recent crop of employee suggestions, and the Suggestion Committee went strutting about the plant emptying their strategically located boxes. Then, as was their custom, they repaired to a secret hideout to remove those suggestions that were either impractical or improper or both, before passing the remainder on for J. J.'s personal perusal.

The suggestion plan had been another brainchild of Andrews and, since its inception it was known to have produced some quite positive results, apart even from the marked reduction in toilet wall graffiti. In fact, from time to time, a worthwhile idea was born in one of those little boxes. And, on such occasions, J. J. took personal delight in bestowing an appropriate award on the suggester, while a dozen other people promptly claimed that the idea had been stolen from them in the first place.

J. J. flicked through the small bundle of suggestions and one neatly typed sheet caught and held her attention. She read it twice. Then she summoned Haley.

As the Director of Engineering marched into the office, J. J., without comment, handed him the sheet of paper. It was headed 'Suggestion re warping of printed circuit boards.'

'Up to last February,' Haley read, 'our printed circuit boards were supplied by Lamitex Company. Then we changed over to the new supplier. It is possible that the new boards are of a poorer quality and are therefore warping under the heat from the solder pot.'

Haley's laugh reverberated through the plant.

'J. J.,' he said tolerantly, 'we're not that stupid. We changed suppliers in February. The problem didn't appear till May.'

'Read on,' suggested J. J.

Haley read on. 'We had a fairly large supply of Lamitex boards in stores at the time we changed suppliers. It is possible that we went on using only the old boards till May and then had an increasing mix of the new ones through June and July. This could have caused the gradual worsening of the problem.'

Haley began to feel that old familiar sinking sensation.

'What do you think?' J. J. asked.

'Naw,' said Haley confidently. 'Impossible.'

'Who evaluated the new supplier?' J. J. enquired gently.

'I'll have to check that out,' Haley answered, modestly refraining from taking the credit due to him. 'Probably O'Keeffe.' Then, recognising the need to cover his rear end, he donned an expression of ferocity.

'By God!' he exclaimed, 'I've had that guy working on this for months. If he's loused it up, he won't know what hit him.'

'Why don't you check it out?' J. J. suggested.

'You bet I will.'

'And let me know the outcome.'

'Sure thing.'

'Because,' said J. J., 'if this guy is right, maybe we should promote him to Engineering Director.'

To Haley that was the most unkindest cut of all and he left the office with heavy heart and bowed head.

As he travelled the long corridor back to his domain, he checked to identify the son of a bitch who was trying to pull the rug from under him.

The note was signed Ignatius P. Freely.

TWENTY-FIVE

It was an animated scene that met the eyes of King and Malone when they returned from a late lunch. Haley had ripped the stores apart until he unearthed some of the old Lamitex circuit boards and Stores personnel were threatening industrial action for disturbance of their peace. On top of that, Andy Sexton had been removed, screaming, to the Medical Centre for sedation after Haley stopped his line in order to feed the old boards into the system.

And now there were the Lamitex boards on their way sedately along the conveyor belt. And there was the line of attentive girls, each stuffing her quota of top-hat transistors, spidery capacitors and gaily colour-coded resistors into the boards as they passed. And there, at the end of the line, close by the bubbling solder pot, was Haley, hovering like an avenging angel, attended nervously by O'Keeffe.

'What's up?' Malone enquired and O'Keeffe wordlessly passed him the suggestion note. When he saw the signature, he looked suspiciously at King, who looked suspiciously innocent.

The first Lamitex board dipped its underside daintily into the molten solder to fix its components firmly in place and, as it moved clear, Haley grabbed it. Heedless of the fact that the smouldering solder was toasting his fingertips to a golden brown, he raised the board to eye level. He began to look most unhappy. He checked the corners on a jig and grew sadder still. Hopefully, he turned his attention

186

to a second board, then a third, but not a trace of a warp was to be seen. A long and pregnant silence followed and then Haley turned violently on O'Keeffe.

'You goddam stupid lame-brain . . . ' he roared, and then he realised that O'Keeffe was no longer present.

Screwing his courage to the sticking point, Haley went and telephoned his boss.

'J. J.,' he announced, 'I've taken over the problem personally from O'Keeffe and I believe I'm on the way to resolving it.'

'Please,' J. J. requested, 'spare me the bullshit. Was it the new supplier?'

'Present indications would appear to point to that possibility,' said Haley, 'but it requires further investigation.'

'Bullshit,' said J. J. again. 'What do you propose to do about it?'

'Firstly,' said Haley, 'I'm going to order a supply of Lamitex boards. Secondly, I'm going to personally re-evaluate the new suppliers. And thirdly,' his voice shook with rage and terror, 'I'm going to fire that stupid son of a bitch.'

'Hold it,' J. J. cautioned. 'Don't do any firing till I give it some thought.'

J. J. promptly called Philadelphia and asked could she please fire Haley immediately. She was so insistent that they finally put her on to Mr de Briggi in person.

'Don't do anything precipitate,' de Briggi told her.

'But,' J. J. pointed out, 'he's a walking disaster.'

'I know that,' de Briggi agreed, 'but he's our longest serving employee. Firing him would be bad for overall morale. Bad for our image.'

'He fouled up the model 660,' J. J. complained, 'and now he's screwed up this PCB deal. Mr de Briggi,' she moaned, 'Phil. He's burying us in scrap.'

'I know. I know,' the president said soothingly.

'Please?' J. J. begged, and de Briggi relented a little.

'I'll tell you what,' he promised, 'I'll get our Accounts boys

187

to look out for an operation where we need a tax write-off.'

'How long will it take?' J. J. asked.

'I can't make any promises,' said de Briggi, and he hung up and considered whether he should fire J. J. because, after all, she was the one with the overall responsibility. But he had just cleared her promotion and if he changed his mind at this point some people might see it as a reflection on his presidential judgement. Not to mention the prospect of a sex discrimination suit.

In an attempt to cover his ass beneath a layer of assertiveness, Haley called J. J. again.

'J. J.,' he said, 'just to let you know. I'm about to fire O'Keeffe over this fiasco.'

'I'd rather you didn't, Paul,' said J. J., quietly ominous.

Haley missed the ominous bit.

'Aw, come on, J. J.,' he argued. 'Why shouldn't I?'

'Because,' said J. J., still gently, 'I'm fucking well telling you.'

To that there was obviously no counter-argument.

'Now about the guy who put in that suggestion. What's his name again?'

'Freely.'

'Have him in my office in ten minutes. I want to present him with a Model 660 in recognition of his contribution.'

'Yes, J. J.,' said Haley meekly.

Anita's persistent cadences finally lured O'Keeffe from his hiding place in the little boys' room. He could hear her sweetly directing him to Mr Haley's office immediately and he decided that he might as well get it over with.

As he entered the office, he put the final touches to his abdication speech and set his jaw in what he considered an aggressive line.

Haley scowled across the desk at O'Keeffe. He noted the pugnacity of the jaw but missed the moisture about the eyes, and he thought better of handing out any abuse in case the guy might turn physical.

'Get me Freely,' he growled.

'Freely?' asked O'Keeffe.

'Are you deaf?' Haley enquired and O'Keeffe shook his head.

'Find him,' Haley commanded. 'The MD wants him in her office in ten minutes.'

'What for?' O'Keeffe asked and Haley took a chance on the violence bit.

'To reward him,' he said, 'for solving your problems.'

O'Keeffe's jaw went more pugnacious and his eyes more moist.

'Go get him, will you, for Chrissakes,' Haley shouted and O'Keeffe left the office, somewhat taken aback at the realisation that he was still in employment.

He sat at his desk and dialled Reception.

'Anita,' he asked, 'will you page Ignatius Freely to call me.'

Anita's voice relayed the message throughout the plant and O'Keeffe's phone rang. But it was not Freely.

'Goddamn it,' Haley roared, 'why don't you get off your ass and go look for the son of a bitch.'

O'Keeffe got off his ass and went as far as the Personnel department.

Liz Donovan was sitting on guard in her new work station outside the three-window office.

'I need to see Brian,' he told her.

Liz sniffed disdainfully, getting a lungful of the solder fumes that hung like a mantle around O'Keeffe.

'He's in Dublin on a course.'

'Oh sweet Jesus!' O'Keeffe prayed.

'The Managerial Grid,' Liz elaborated, 'whatever that may be. He'll be back on Friday.'

'For the love and honour of God, Liz,' O'Keeffe besought her, 'can you tell me where I might find Ignatius Freely?'

'He works in Engineering,' Liz told him.

'No he doesn't!'

'Yes he does.'

'I work in bloody Engineering,' O'Keeffe pointed out shrilly, 'I should bloody well know.'

'What do you want him for anyway?' Liz asked.

''Tis the Managing Director wants him,' O'Keeffe said, and Liz instantly gave the matter a higher priority.

'Well,' she said, 'I'm certain he works in Engineering.'

'He works in Production,' O'Keeffe said.

'Engineering,' Liz responded emphatically.

'No, he doesn't!' O'Keeffe bawled.

Liz shrugged her shoulder pads dismissively and O'Keeffe took a moment to calm his bouncing Adam's apple.

'Would you ever mind checking the files?' he asked her.

'Oh, very well.' She glided over to the four-drawer filing cabinet at the edge of her desk and unlocked it. 'But I know for a fact that he works in Engineering.'

With an effort, O'Keeffe held his peace as her scarlet fingernails trotted through the personnel folders.

Meanwhile J. J. was on the phone again to Haley.

'What's keeping Freely?' she asked.

'We're running the guy down,' Haley remarked.

'What do you mean, running him down?'

'It's a big plant,' Haley said, and immediately regretted his daring. 'I mean,' he amended quickly, 'I got O'Keeffe looking for him.'

'Maybe,' suggested J. J., 'you should try doing something yourself.'

Haley thought it better not to answer back.

'You got another ten minutes,' said J. J. very distinctly, and hung up.

Garda O'Shaughnessy came plodding into the lobby and approached the reception desk.

'I'm here on official business, Missie,' he informed Anita.

Liz turned back to O'Keeffe. She looked quite pale around the gills.

'I . . . I can't find him!' she confessed.

'What do you mean?' O'Keeffe asked.

'He isn't in our files,' her limpid eyes grew moist and fogged up her oversized designer glasses.

'Good Christ!' said O'Keeffe. 'You must have him filed out of place.'

And the moisture in Liz's eyes evaporated instantly under the hot glare that she turned on him.

'Are you suggesting,' she enquired, 'that I don't know my job?'

Further along the corridor, Andrews leaned out of his office, disturbed by the commotion.

'What's up?' he demanded.

'I'm trying to find Ignatius Freely,' O'Keeffe told him.

'He doesn't work in this department.'

'I know that.'

'He works in Engineering,' Liz piped up.

'No he doesn't!' O'Keeffe's Adam's apple was now threatening to pop right out of his gullet.

'Did you check the files?' Andrews asked and Liz nodded dolefully.

'Did you check the alphabetical register?'

Liz nodded once more.

'According to the records,' she said, 'he doesn't work here at all.'

'You're crazy,' said O'Keeffe, living dangerously, 'everyone knows Freely.' He turned towards Andrews. 'A tall thin fellow. With long hair.'

Andrews nodded.

'Yeah, I know him.'

'With a Cork accent.'

'Let me try Payroll,' said Andrews and he went back into his office and dialled the Accounts Department. Liz pranced indignantly into Collins's office and began a frantic search

191

of his files.

O'Keeffe wrung his hands and waited restlessly for news.

In Reception Anita looked curiously up at the huge law enforcer.

'Mr Andrews's phone is busy right now. Will you take a seat and I'll try again in a minute.'

Garda O'Shaughnessy was not inclined to take a seat while on duty so he patrolled the lobby, moving stolidly back and forth between the main door and the entrance to the offices.

Andrews got Phil Ashe from Accounts on the phone.

'Phil,' he said, 'we're doing a check on the salary history of Ignatius Freely.'

'Freely . . . Freely . . . ' said Ashe, delving into his memory bank.

'Could you get someone to drop me over his payroll file?' Andrews asked.

'Right you are, Merv,' agreed Ashe. 'I'll send it over after lunch.'

'Could you do it now? It's urgent.'

Ashe went into a long spiel about the pressures on his department but Andrews cut him short.

'Phil,' he said, 'I'm not asking for a five year plan. Just one small file.'

'All right. All right,' said Ashe ungraciously. 'I'll send it right over.'

'Thank you very much,' said Andrews and hung up.

Phil Ashe called to Bridie Power, the payroll clerk.

'Bridie,' he said, 'Personnel have screwed up their records again. They want a look at our file on Ignatius Freely.'

Bridie nodded.

'Will you drop it over to Merv Andrews right away,' Ashe asked, and Bridie nodded again. The awful responsibility of her office, and the confidentiality of the information she handled, had almost deprived her of the power of speech.

She started to flick expertly through her files.

Andrews's phone rang. It was Anita.

'Mr Andrews,' she told him, 'I have Garda O'Shaughnessy here in the lobby.'

'Who?'

'Garda O'Shaughnessy. He wants to see you.'

'Me?' Andrews's voice went suddenly falsetto. 'What does he want to see *me* about?'

'He says it's official business.'

'Holy shit,' said Andrews but he said it to himself. 'OK, send him on in.'

Haley was going about like a roaring lion, seeking whom he might devour, preferably O'Keeffe, when he met King outside the print room.

'Where the hell were you?' he greeted.

'When?' King asked brightly.

It wasn't as simple a question to answer as it sounded and Haley bypassed it.

'Did you see O'Keeffe?' he demanded.

'When?' asked King.

'Do you know,' Haley tried again, aiming at preciseness, 'where Ignatius Freely is at this point in time?'

'Freely?'

'Yeah, goddam it. Freely.'

'If I see him, I'll tell him you're looking for him,' King promised.

'Tell him the MD wants to see him in her office.'

'Can I say for what?' King asked.

'To give him a goddam award,' said Haley, 'for his suggestion about the PCBs.'

Haley took off again, seeking a candidate more palatable for devouring.

In the payroll office, Bridie was having palpitations. She could find no record of Ignatius P. Freely. Quickly, she passed the information and the palpitations on to Phil Ashe and, together, they began a hysterical search through folders, tax returns, holiday schedules, shuddering in unison at the horrible fate that lay ahead should the auditors ever discover that they had mislaid one warm body.

It was Phil Ashe on the phone again.

'Merv,' he said quaveringly, 'it may take a bit longer than I expected to dig out Freely's file.'

'Why, for Chrissakes?'

'Bridie isn't around at the moment,' Ashe looked earnestly at said Bridie. 'She's the one who knows where everything is.'

'You mean,' Andrews yelled, 'you've screwed up your records again.'

'Haven't *you*?'

Andrews was about to let loose a string of profanities when he looked up and saw the doorway filled, top to bottom and side to side, by the figure of Garda O'Shaughnessy. Quickly, he got his smile back into position and waved the garda in.

'Come in, Officer,' he greeted. 'Come in.' Then to Ashe, 'Get it to me as quickly as you can,' he said and hung up.

'Take a seat, Officer,' Andrews suggested, but the Garda shook his head politely. It would not be proper to sit on one of those comfortable chairs and he on official business.

'So . . . ' said Andrews, 'what can I do for you?'

'I have here,' the garda patted his top left pocket, 'a summons.'

Andrews's smile thinned.

'For an employee of this company.'

Andrews relaxed a little. At least it wasn't for him.

'Drunk and disorderly,' O'Shaughnessy intoned, 'disturbing the peace. And,' he added, 'giving out a false address.'

'Wouldn't it be more appropriate,' Andrews pointed out, 'to do this at his home, rather than at his place of work. Or hers . . . ' he added mindful of the affirmative action bullshit.

'Gave a wrong address, you see.' The policeman stood towering over everything in the office, feet planted firmly on the carpet, hands clasped behind his back, face devoid of expression. Andrews felt very threatened.

'The incident took place,' O'Shaughnessy said, 'on the morning of the nineteenth of October at approximately three fifteen a.m., following a party held by your Company at the Lakeside Hotel.'

'Who was it?' Andrews asked. 'I'll have him – or her – paged.'

From his top pocket, the Garda extracted an official-looking document.

'The name of the individual concerned is . . . ' He read from the document, ' . . . Ignatius Freely.'

'Igna-' Andrews's mind went blank. His smile went away. He aged visibly.

Garda O'Shaughnessy waited patiently.

After a moment Andrews came back to life. 'Excuse me,' he bleated and jumped from his seat. At the doorway he paused a moment. 'I'll have to trace his whereabouts.'

The garda nodded and Andrews took off.

Outside in the corridor he saw O'Keeffe make a frantic grab at Willie King, who was on his way to somewhere or other. 'Where the hell is Freely?' O'Keeffe demanded.

'Just what I wanted to know,' Andrews chipped in.

'How would I know?' replied King.

'Do you know what department he works in?'

'Personnel, I think.'

'No, he bloody well doesn't!' Liz squealed from inside the office.

'You mean you can't trace him?' King asked innocently.

'Why the hell,' wailed O'Keeffe, 'do you think we're here pissing in our trousers?'

'Come to think of it', King said thoughtfully, 'I haven't seen him around lately. I wonder if he might have quit?'

'Quit?' said O'Keeffe hopefully.

'We'd have it on our records,' said Andrews, shaking his head.

'Remember the night his engagement was broken off?' King asked.

'What about it?'

'He phoned me that night,' said King, 'and, as far as I can remember, he said he was going away forever.'

'Going away?' said Andrews, hopefully. 'Forever?'

'I wasn't too sober at the time,' King admitted, 'but I think he said he couldn't bear to face his colleagues after the shame of it all.'

'You know,' said O'Keeffe, getting brighter by the second, 'I haven't seen him around for a while either.'

'That's it!' Andrews said, suddenly confident again. 'He quit! Liz!' he roared, and Liz stuck a slightly pink nose past the door.

'Liz,' said Andrews, 'you'll find Freely in our terminated files.'

'I won't,' she informed him. 'I tried.'

'Well, that's where he should be,' said Andrews.

'If it is,' she said, 'nobody bothered to send us a termination slip.'

'Well,' said King, 'I've got things to do.'

King went on his merry way, leaving a long and meaningful look hanging between O'Keeffe and Andrews. Decisively, Andrews marched into Collins's office and found a termination slip and within ninety seconds Ignatius Freely's employment had been terminated for personal reasons, effective the twentieth of October with a notation that all Company property and tools issued to him had been returned and that he would not be considered suitable for re-hire.

O'Keeffe grabbed the phone and got through to Haley.

'Freely quit last month,' he said, before Haley had time to deliver any broadsides.

'He quit?'

'Yes,' said O'Keeffe.

'What the hell took you so long to find out?'

'Ah,' said O'Keeffe, 'you know the Personnel Department.'

Andrews was too shaken to take umbrage. Hastily, he added one more comment to the termination slip: 'No forwarding address.' Then he headed back towards his office to tell his visitor the trail had gone cold.

Haley passed the word along to J. J.

'And,' the Managing Director commented, 'it took you forty-five minutes to find that out.'

'I should have known better than to let O'Keeffe handle it,' Haley explained. 'J. J.,' he pleaded, 'I gotta fire the guy. He's nothing but trouble.'

'He won't trouble you much longer, if I can help it,' J. J. promised, and Haley hung up feeling better than he should have, because he thought J. J. meant it one way, and J. J. really meant it another.

And then, mercifully, came the call that made J. J.'s day. It was Williams, reporting that he had swung the deal with both Marketing and Personnel, duly signed and approved by four levels of management. Half a million Model 660s a year for four years at an even better price than J. J. had hoped for. A major revision of production plans and profit plans was called for.

'We'll get right on it,' J. J. assured her leader and immediately issued a summons to her managers to drop everything and convene for some good news for a change.

TWENTY-SIX

When Worldwide Electronics first set up shop in Ballyderra, they installed a full matching set of American managers to whip the natives into shape. From the start, however, Management took pains to give assurances that those natives who showed proper respect for their superiors and a willingness to work their butts off could, in time, aspire to high office.

But the years rolled by and, as each American was shipped home at the end of his sentence, he was promptly replaced by another of the same ilk and so the top line remained securely in the grip of expatriates. It was not that anyone had lied in their dentures, neither was it for want of promising local talent. The truth of the matter was that the Company had discovered in Ballyderra an ideal patch for the temporary transplantation of certain managerial species.

Firstly, there were those people suspected of possessing ability, like J. J., and who seemed destined for high places. For this select few, some overseas battleground experience was considered a must. Then there were the ones who, like Haley, had demonstrated a fine consistency in making a balls of everything they touched. For them, Ballyderra was a new-found limbo to which they could be consigned until a decision was made whether to can them or kick them upstairs out of harm's way.

In one of his many idle moments, King had made a study of the frequency of American turnover at the plant, and found that the average individual stay worked out at three years.

'Which,' he expounded, 'is the optimum period. One year finding out where the guy before you hid his skeletons. Then a year to create your own foul-ups and the third year to hide them from the next guy.'

And so when, on a certain crisp November day, Jennifer J. Carey visited MacNamara's jewellery shop in Parnell Street and ordered two Waterford decanters, the word went out that the gifts might be intended for some Americans who were coming due for deportation.

Then began the time of the gamblers. J. J.'s three year stint was just about up and, since she seemed to have some idea of what she was about, she was likely to be in demand elsewhere. The betting on her was two to one. Andrews had been around just three years and had done little either good or bad, which made him third favourite at five to two. Haley was long odds at five to one, mainly because he had been at Ballyderra for just over a year and would still be in a position to blame most of his mistakes on his predecessor. But the hot favourite at two to one on was Myles K. O'Shee, who had proved he couldn't really cut the mustard by throwing a series of nervous breakdowns during the strike. The starter's flag was up and all of Ballyderra knew it except, of course, the runners themselves.

But then, a few days after J. J.'s visit to the jewellers, a dark horse entered the field.

Only one thing on this earth gave Doc Roche more pleasure than examining female patients and that was traditional Irish music. And so, when he learned that an antique aunt had passed away leaving him a sizeable pot of money he decided, after some soul-searching, to forego his secondary pleasures and devote his remaining years and energy to collecting folk music.

When this news reached the gambling fraternity, it was agreed that the betting would apply only to any departing Americans. In the unlikely event that one of the decanters was destined for Doc's sideboard it would not count. But neither would it affect the odds on the other runners.

Doc's impending retirement was as good an excuse as any for a booze-up and Collins co-opted King and Malone to form an organising committee.

They convened in Collins's new confession corner. Malone was deputed to book the function room at the Lakeside and they pondered at some length on the matter of a suitable parting gift from friends and colleagues. 'I've got it!' King exclaimed.

'What?' enquired Malone.

'I know just the thing to give Doc.'

'What is it?' asked Collins.

'I'll organise it,' King told them. 'Just leave it to me.'

They left it to King, though they knew they should have known better.

'Do you happen to be going into Limerick on Saturday?' King asked Collins.

'Probably.'

'Right you are,' said King. 'I'll arrange for you to pick it up.'

King and Malone got up to take their leave.

'Jim,' said Collins casually, 'can you hang on a minute?'

King and Malone exchanged raised eyebrows as King left.

Malone turned back, looking puzzled.

– Definitely confession corner for this –

'I won't keep you a minute,' Collins assured Malone as he ushered him to a chair by the glass-topped table. 'Tell me . . . ' Collins got straight to the point, ' . . . have you ever given any thought to a change of career?'

Malone wondered what the hell this was leading to. As far as he knew, he had done nothing to warrant getting canned.

'Not more than two or three times a day,' he answered.

– If he doesn't watch it he'll end up in the shit like his buddy King –

'Most of the time,' Malone went on, at least half-

200

truthfully, 'I think about having a fishing boat of my own out of Castletownbere.'

'Can we talk strictly off the record here?' Collins asked.

'Sure.'

'It's highly confidential.'

Collins got up and shut his door carefully.

Malone was now more puzzled than ever.

'Jim,' Collins lowered his voice, 'we're going to see some major organisational changes around here any day now.'

'You mean the decanters J. J. ordered?'

'Partly. But I've got approval to hire someone for my old job. Personnel and Training Manager.'

'Ah,' said Malone astutely, 'they're shipping old Andrews out?'

'No comment.'

'Couldn't happen to a nicer guy.'

'Would you be interested in the job?'

'What job?' then Malone's penny dropped. 'A job in Personnel?' he asked incredulously.

Collins nodded.

'You think I'm crazy?' Malone began to laugh. 'Isn't it bad enough working in Engineering?'

'Don't just shoot it down like that,' Collins urged. 'Think about it.'

'What the hell do I know about personnel work?'

'I didn't know anything about it when I came aboard,' Collins pointed out. 'I came straight from teaching.'

'That's all very well, but I'm . . . '

'And not only did I have to learn about personnel work,' Collins cut in, 'I had to learn about the Company, the organisation, the industrial scene on top of that. You've been here for four years. You'd be off to a flying start.'

'You're out of your mind, Brian. I wasn't cut out for that kind of work.'

'I think you are,' Collins insisted. 'You're very well liked, you know.'

'Since when,' Malone asked, 'is being liked a qualification for Personnel?'

'It would mean a good salary increase. And a two-window office. You'd learn the job a hell of a lot quicker than I did.'

'Forget it, Brian,' Malone stood up. 'You're talking to the wrong guy.'

Standing, he was just a little taller than Collins sitting. He pulled his suit jacket down in place around his hips. 'But thanks for the kind thought,' he said as he went to the door.

'Promise me you'll think about it,' Collins asked and Malone shrugged in a manner that didn't say yes or didn't say no.

'I'll get back to you about it in a day or two,' Collins said to Malone's back. 'And remember, this is highly confidential.'

'Absolutely,' Malone assured him. He held the doorknob, 'Open or closed?' he asked.

'Open, please.'

Malone went on his way.

– *You're not going to let him off the hook* –

Collins went back and sat behind the desk. The priority folder lay on his desk, neglected, accusing.

He checked his page-a-week calendar to see what else was in store. The rest of the day was clear of appointments.

– *Thank God for small mercies* –

The following morning was highlighted with a black cross.

His father's anniversary.

– *Nine o'clock mass at the Friary the Ma, Frank, Eileen, Uncle Bill they'll all be there Father James will say the mass great old stick, Father James . . . you were the only one the Da could count on to smuggle the drink to him . . . you refused him*

that one time . . . for his own good . . . and he turns that mournful,
hurt look on you . . . Jesus, but he knew how to blackmail you
with that look and you never said no to him again and then
when he died you felt so damn guilty because of all the drink you
got for him until Father James put it to you that you might have
been helping the Da to live because at that stage his life wasn't
worth living without the whiskey . . . that consoled you . . . a
bit, anyway –

Collins drew a deep breath and turned to his priority
file.

TWENTY-SEVEN

When a westerly gale sends the rain stampeding through O'Connell Street's Georgian canyon in Limerick, it is a good place not to be, and both wind and rain were giving of their diabolical best when Collins hit town. It was almost five o'clock and the traffic was tensing up for its rush-hour hysterics, while people in the lengthening bus queues huddled for shelter behind each other's resentful backs.

Collins squirmed Lucy's Mini into a gap in the line of cars illegally parked by the kerb and sprinted across the street to the drapery shop directly opposite. Inside, he found himself confronted by a small, much-lined, presumably female figure which tendered an expressionless smile of welcome.

'I was asked,' Collins announced, 'to collect a package for Mr Willie King.'

'Oh yes indeed.' The lady showed a little more interest. 'For Mr King. Will you come this way, please.'

She led the way into an incredibly untidy room at the back of the shop. The air was heavy with the smell of new cloth, laced with mustiness and damp.

'Follow me,' she invited, and went skipping lightly among crushed hatboxes, loose cloth bales and sundry dismembered display models. Collins tagged cumbrously along, wincing a little as he felt a model's skull crunch beneath his inadvertent heel.

The lady was waiting for him at the far end of the room. 'There you are now,' she said, pointing downwards, and

Collins's eyes began to protrude quite noticeably.

Her outstretched finger was aimed at a display model, feminine gender, laid full length on the floor, quite bare, and as far as his abashed eye could tell, perfect in every detail.

– *Jesus, Mary and Joseph!* –

'I call her Beth,' the lady said but Collins failed to acknowledge the introduction.

'That?' he asked after an indecent interval, and the lady nodded.

– *King! The bastard. I'll have his balls for this* –

He had just decided to get his ass out of there fast when he caught the gleam in the old lady's eye, and it told him she was waiting sadistically to see his nerve snap.

– *Don't let them best you, Killer* –

He decided to hang in there, and that was his first mistake.

'Would you mind,' he asked calmly, 'wrapping it up?'

The little woman eyed Beth's six foot of undulations; then she eyed Collins.

'Is it joking you are?' she enquired, and her tone was unmistakably rhetorical.

But Collins's back was now well and truly up. Decisively, he bent and took a firm grip on Beth's shapely hips. She was rigid and quite heavy, but he managed to hoist her and secure her horizontally beneath his arm.

He looked the lady squarely in the eye, took two dignified steps toward the door and panicked. Out through the shop he bolted and out on to the street with Beth tucked under his arm, and that was his second mistake.

Up to this point, his new-found friend had been quite compliant but the moment the cold wind struck her unprotected torso she turned nasty. Without a word of warning, she spun like a windmill in the gale and would undoubtedly have thrown Collins right through the shop window had not her dainty feet come in violent contact with the midriff of a passing gentleman.

'Whooof!' remarked the passing gentleman vehemently, and he stopped passing and went down bassackward on the wet pavement.

Collins regained his balance and quickly concluded that to pause for an exchange of pleasantries with the no-longer-passing gentleman would be pointless and possibly hazardous. Urged on by the ringing cheers from the bus queue and the determined efforts of the motorists to grind him beneath their wheels, he raced across the street to the car.

By now, Beth was wet and slippery and showing ever-increasing signs of agitation. He stood her upright against the car while he unpocketed his keys and she promptly dived to one side in an effort to escape. But he was too quick for her. He caught her by the neck and hauled her upright again. Then, to prevent further efforts to break away, he pressed his heavy body full against her, pinning her helplessly against the side of the car.

This touch of intimacy brought a favourable reaction from Beth and her struggles ceased, giving Collins the opportunity to get the door open. Nor did she raise any protest as his hands slid down her back and took a firm grip on her rounded buttocks. But when he suddenly tilted her sideways to propel her into the car and a particularly violent gust of wind struck her below deck, she turned on him savagely. With an expert flick, she threw him on his back across the car bonnet and laid herself on top of him in a posture that was quite immodest.

– *Oh, God. What did I ever do to deserve this!* –

At this point in the proceedings, several people in the bus queue turned their gazes elsewhere lest they might take pleasure in the scene. A few there were who offered ribald counsel but it was plain from their accents and demeanour that they were blow-ins, and not true natives of that ancient and honourable city.

The car door slammed shut, and Collins whispered in Beth's ear.

'Fuck you,' said he and it came straight from the heart.

– LISTEN TO YOU! –

– *Fuck you too!* –

Then he launched his counter-offensive. With a grunt and a heave and a mighty flailing of legs, he rolled his adversary over on to her back, and took up a commanding position astride her body, gripping her fiercely between his powerful knees. From this dominant position he paused to review the situation. He decided to call in outside help.

He looked about him. Saw a friendly face approaching.

'Would you ever,' he pleaded, 'hold on to this one till I get the door open?'

The friendly face gazed on the erotic tableau and quickly averted his eyes.

'Please?' Collins begged.

'Ju think I'm a bloody prevert or something?' the face demanded, and away with its owner in search of a priest or a garda or someone to put a stop to this public display of debauchery which could well bring down fire and brimstone on the entire innocent city.

Collins knew then that this was an ordeal which he must face alone and unaided. He drew a long, deep breath and lay forward on top of Beth, grasping her in a passionate embrace. Then, smooth as a well-rehearsed dance movement, he rolled off the bonnet and landed himself and herself, still locked together, on their feet again near the door.

Again he managed to get the door open and this time he succeeded in outsmarting both Beth and the wind by keeping her on a low trajectory.

The Mini was one of those two-door things, with tip-forward front seats to enable rear passengers to slip their discs when entering or alighting, and it took some strenuous convolutions to get her all in. But finally, there she was, stretched diagonally across the car, her head jammed against the far corner of the rear window, her heels resting on the steering wheel, full frontally upward, and looking as if butter wouldn't melt in her mouth.

– *Got you, you bloody bitch* –

For a long, triumphant moment he stood there, leering maliciously down at his vanquished foe, and then suddenly the sweet taste of victory curdled in his mouth.

–*Oh, suffering Jesus!* –

In spite of her violent and unwarranted struggles, he had forced her to bend to his will. The problem now was how to bend his large frame into the driving seat.

He tried to push her feet over off the steering wheel, but her body was unyielding and her head was too firmly jammed against the back window. He tried to squeeze in beneath her but quickly realised that he was not sufficiently collapsible. For a brief moment, he considered attempting to drive while sitting astride those delectable legs but he abandoned the idea because of the danger of personal injury in trying to reach the pedals. He was well and truly stymied and he knew it.

Collins stepped back and, with the rain cascading down inside his clothes and despair in his heart, he enquired once more of Heaven what he had done to deserve such tribulations. As if in answer to his prayer, the solution came to him in a flash.

Like all brilliant solutions, it was perfectly obvious once you had it. All he had to do was take her out again and insert her from the other side. That way, her feet would be resting on the back of the passenger seat and thus leave the driver's side free of encumbrance.

With a sigh of relief, he slid her smoothly out of the car. Too late, he realised that he had given her an opening. With the help of a specially strong wind-squall, she whipped around and flung him once more on his back across the bonnet and followed up by throwing herself forcefully on top of him. Pressing her advantage, she began to gouge his right eye out with her nose or something.

The plight of a man beaten to his knees, his spirit broken in smithereens, is best not dwelt upon. Suffice it to say that Collins gave forth a great wail of anguish that could be heard for miles around. Then he clasped Beth desperately to his breast and went staggering back across the street and into the shop.

This time there was no one behind the counter and he bore his heavy burden into the back room. He stood her carefully upright. He cast a wild glare about but of the old lady there was no sign. Then very deliberately and with malice aforethought, he drew back his strong right leg and, with all the force of his pent-up anger, he planted a mighty kick on Beth's inviting bottom. And that was his final mistake of the day.

It was a well-aimed kick, sure enough, and Beth sailed halfway across the room before coming in to a perfect three point landing. But even in that fierce moment of exultation, Collins realised that his opponent had the last word, because, in his highly emotional state, he had failed to reckon on her solidity. For a long time he stood there on one leg, howling with the excruciating pain of a dislocated ankle.

When, at last, Collins hobbled back out onto the street, the rainclouds had exhausted their resources and the sun was raising steam from the pavements to provide them with further ammunition. The sky was a disarmingly innocent blue, the rush-hour traffic had been drained away and neatly tucked behind his windscreen wiper was a parking summons.

As he drove disconsolately west on O'Connell Street, the big voice began to reassert itself.

– You made a right disgrace of yourself –

– *Provocation . . . there was extreme provocation* –

– Confession! –

− All right I'll run in to the Jesuits −

The big voice was mollified, but only for a moment.

− AND WHERE ARE YOU GOING TO PARK? −

− In the Crescent in front of the church −

− THERE'S NEVER ANY PARKING SPACE IN THE CRESCENT −

By this stage in the argument he had reached the Crescent and, sure enough, the parked cars were bumper-locked along the yellow lines at the kerb on both sides of the street.

− WHAT DID I TELL YOU! −

− We'll find a spot further on −

− YOU'RE TRYING TO BACK OUT OF IT −

− No I'm not −

− WHO DO YOU THINK YOU'RE FOOLING! −

He was passing the O'Connell statue in front of the Jesuits when, without warning, a black Mercedes swung sharply out from the kerb and cut across his bows.

− Christ! −

Only his quick reflexes prevented a nasty accident. He jammed on the brakes and spun the wheel sharply to the left.

− IT'S A SIGN! −

His evasive action had skidded him right into the parking spot just vacated by the Mercedes.

− WELL? − THE BIG VOICE DEMANDED TRIUMPHANTLY.

− I'm going I'm going −

The little light was on over Father Martin's confessional and there was only one person waiting. A woman in a grey coat on devout knees outside the door nearest to the altar.

− Good . . . Father Martin is the best of them −

− ALWAYS THE EASY WAY OUT −

He knelt outside the penitential door. The aroma of last night's incense and fresh furniture polish added to the devotional air of the dim, lofty interior. He could hear the low hiss from inside the box as some poor sinner unburdened his soul.

He made the sign of the cross and began his preparation.

– *I confess to Almighty God* –

– OH YOU'RE ON THE SLIPPERY SLOPE, BOYO –

–*And to you, my brothers and sisters* –

– SWEARING RIGHT, LEFT AND CENTRE –

– *in what I have done and what I have failed to do* –

– AND ENTERTAINING IMPURE THOUGHTS –

– *I didn't entertain them . . . all the angels and saints*

– AND THE LIES –

– *Officious lies only . . . to pray for me to the Lord* –

– THAT'S RIGHT RATIONALISE EVERYTHING –

The confessional door opened slowly and a boy, not more than seven, made his escape. Blonde hair slicked back smoothly. Angelic face aglow with relief at having offloaded his awful burden of sin.

Collins eased himself into the confined darkness of the box.

Father Martin, SJ sat cramped in his section of the confessional and helped himself to another pinch of snuff, his prophylactic against the germs and odours that his penitents might bring with them into the confined space along with their stained souls.

He heard the door on his right open and someone knelt heavily on the other side of the partition.

'O God be merciful to me, a sinner,' the priest ejaculated to himself, as he always did before sliding back the shutter.

'Bless me, Father, for I have sinned,' the penitent opened up.

Father Martin knew this lad. Not by name or even by appearance, because he always kept his eyes conscientiously averted from the dividing grille. But he was good at voices and accents, and he could tell that this was the lad from somewhere along the Limerick-Kerry border, whose mode of speech had been modified by several years of exposure to other dialects, probably at University. He could tell that the penitent was large because the voice came through the top portion of the grille.

'Yes, my child,' Father Martin responded.

'It's two weeks since my last confession.'

Hmm, said the priest to himself, it's usually a month for this lad. Something's up.

Collins drew a deep breath and it all came out together.

'I've neglected my morning and evening prayers, I've used bad language and taken the Holy Name on numerous occasions and . . . I've had impure thoughts five times.'

He actually keeps score, said the voice in the priest's head.

'Yes, my child,' said Father Martin again. 'Now about the bad language. You know it's not only sinful, but it can also give scandal to others.'

'Well,' said the big lad, 'generally I just say it in my mind.'

In the darkness the priest nodded thoughtfully several times.

'I see,' he said, 'but it's still sinful, you know.'

'I know.'

'And the impure thoughts. Were they about someone in particular?'

'No, Father. Well, yes, actually. They were mainly about my wife.'

Father Martin took time to ponder on this and the big lad felt the need to elaborate.

'She's pregnant, you see.'

The good priest didn't really see, but that was all right as long as the lad was truly repentant for whatever evil he thought he had done.

'Anything else, my child?' he asked.

'No, Father.'

'Very well, then. For your penance say five Hail Marys and pray for the strength to resist future temptations.'

'Yes, Father.'

The lad launched into his Act of Contrition, while the priest administered absolution, thinking that, if all of his other penitents were as scruple-driven as this lad, life would be very dull indeed. The lad would have made a fine priest, though not a Jesuit. He'd be a bit too innocent for the order.

It was raining again when Collins came out of the church. He made a jinking dash across the street and it was only after he got the engine started that he noticed, nestling on the windscreen, his second parking ticket of the day.

– DON'T SAY IT! – and, conscious of his freshly shriven soul, he didn't.

TWENTY-EIGHT

Malone was one of those people who are never at ease unless they have some cause for worry, and right now his uppermost source of comforting concern was none other than his friend King.

Over the past few weeks, King's normally erratic behaviour pattern had undergone a noticeable change. The guy had taken to coming in at night in an unacceptably sober condition and going out in the mornings with equally unacceptable punctuality. Worse still, he had bought himself a whole new wardrobe and now went about his work fully suited, collared and tied. Worst of all, he had abandoned his favourite pastime of adding daily to the trials and tribulations of Paul Haley.

Now, here was Doc's retirement party in full flood, and there was the son of a bitch with one arm draped along the top of the piano and the other one proprietorially around Anita Merry's waist. Wearing a blue double-breasted blazer that Malone had not seen before and giving his full attention to Collins, who was rendering his own arrangement of Liszt's Hungarian Rhapsody with a boogie-woogie left hand.

The performance came to a sudden, crashing climax and Collins modestly acknowledged the applause.

'Jesus,' said King, 'what's a guy with your talent doing in this shitty outfit?'

It wasn't often anyone found himself on the receiving end of a sincere compliment from King, and Collins tried hard to conceal his pleasure. Then he caught Jennifer Carey's signal across the room.

Collins limped to the platform at the end of the hall and managed to persuade Captain's son, Kenny the disco king, to hold off a while from beating people's brains into submission with his music.

'Ladies and gentlemen,' Collins bawled, 'could we have a bit of shush!' The shush was slow in coming and he yelled even louder. 'Will ye for the love and honour of God, belt up a minute.'

– GOOD THING LUCY ISN'T HERE! –

The heartfelt plea and the extra decibels got him the partial attention of most of the celebrants.

'Ladies and gentlemen,' Collins proceeded, and his words were just slightly out of focus due to the unaccustomed amount of drink he had inside him, 'we are gathered here this evening to pay a final tribute to one of our most respected colleagues.'

– MAKING AN EXHIBITION OF YOURSELF! –

'And may he be in Heaven,' Malone shouted, 'half an hour before the devil knows he's dead.'

– THAT'S EXACTLY WHAT SHE'D SAY –

'I am referring, of course,' Collins continued, 'to none other than our esteemed doctor, Kieran Roche.'

There was some scattered, drunken applause.

'And here to say a few words, ladies and gentlemen,' his voice broke with emotion or inebriation or something, 'is our respected and revered Managing Director, Miz J. J. Carey.'

Amid the applause, Jennifer J. Carey mounted the platform. She looked splendidly managerial in her pearl-grey, not-too-tightly-fitting jacket and skirt, though she had allowed herself a splash of colour in the form of a scarlet silk blouse. Her burnished hair hung in soft waves almost to her shoulders. No noticeable make-up, as usual, but everyone agreed that she was something to see.

215

For some reason, Collins felt obliged to shake the great woman's hand fervently.

'Ladies and gentlemen,' J. J. began, and then corrected herself. 'Fellow employees, I have a number of surprise announcements to make this evening. By a strange coincidence, I have just learned that we are about to lose, not just one colleague, but three.'

That was a lowdown lie for starters, because she had got the OK from Headquarters several days before. 'Yes,' she went on, smiling as if she meant it, 'I've been informed that two members of our management team are to be transferred immediately to other areas of our great Company. One is about to experience all the charms of the East in our manufacturing facility in Taiwan. And that lucky guy is none other than our Engineering Director, Paul K. Haley.'

There was a silence, brief and slightly stunned. Then came a loud, ringing cheer, not so much at Haley's good fortune as at Ireland's and who the hell cared about what lay in store for Taiwan.

'And secondly,' J. J. continued, 'in recognition of all he has done here in Ireland, Mervyn P. Andrews is moving back to Headquarters to take up the position of Director of International Compensation and Benefits. And with a job like that, we'd all better be very nice to him.'

There was another brief bout of applause.

And thus was demonstrated the depth of J. J.'s duplicity. Cunningly, she had decided to hold back the announcements until Doc's party so that she could include all three men in one general valediction and so spare herself and her audience all that nauseating crap about illustrious careers and significant contributions. She took a sip from her lemonade for lubrication lest the words might stick in her craw.

It was obvious from their lack of expression that both Haley and Andrews had been given the good news in advance.

'Therefore,' J. J. went on, 'we are losing not one good man but three, and I'd like to take advantage of this opportunity to wish Paul and Merv and Doc every success in their future endeavours.'

She paused to permit applause, well pleased at the manner in which she had eased herself through the situation.

'Shite,' Malone whispered to King, 'who's going to get Haley's job?'

King shrugged.

'Another Yank we'll have to break in.'

'You'd never know,' said King.

'I understand,' J. J. continued, 'that arrangements have been made to present Doc with an appropriate memento of his years among us, and so it is now my pleasant duty to present a farewell gift to Paul and Merv.' She called their names: 'Paul! Merv!'

The two men made their way to the platform.

'On behalf of the Management,' J. J. intoned rapidly, 'I have great pleasure in presenting you with these beautiful pieces of Waterford Crystal, and I hope they will always remind you of your brief but eventful stay in this ancient and beautiful country.'

J. J. shook hands with Andrews and Haley as the gifts changed hands. Haley looked at the ship's decanter with its delicate pattern twinkling under the lights and wondered what the hell it was.

'Speech,' cried Phil Ashe, and the cry was taken up by several other drunks.

Mercifully, J. J. nipped that idea in the bud.

'That's not all,' she proclaimed as she produced a couple of sheets of paper from somewhere. 'I have some other good news.' A Freudian slip, surely. 'Let me read out a couple of announcements that I'll be circulating to you all tomorrow morning. The first one is from Mr Philip de Briggi, Chief Executive Officer.' She cleared her throat and began to read.

Fellow Employees

I am very pleased to announce that our Company has acquired an electronic manufacturing facility near Madrid, Spain. This new operation will report to Miz Jennifer J. Carey who will also continue in charge of our highly successful Irish operation. Miz Carey's new title will be Vice-President of Operations, West Europe.

This time the cheers were louder and more genuine. And this time the announcement was news to all except Collins. News even to Haley and Andrews.

'Now,' J. J. called out, 'for the second announcement, which I'll also be issuing tomorrow. This one comes from me personally.' She referred to a second sheet of paper:

Fellow Employees,

Arising from the acquisition of the new facilities in Spain and the transfer of two key managers, I am pleased to announce the following organisational changes:

Mr Brian Collins is promoted to the position of Director of Human Resources, West Europe and will be responsible to me for the Personnel functions in both countries.

There was another burst of silence, followed by the loudest cheer of all and they crowded around Collins, trying to beat the shit out of him with delight. It was clear from the slippage of Andrews's smile that he hadn't known about *this* one either.

'Furthermore . . .' J. J. continued reading and the cheering subsided, 'I am happy to announce that the position of Engineering Director, vacated by Paul K. Haley, will be filled by William A. King.'

This time even Collins was taken by surprise.

– That's why she didn't want me to consider King for the

Personnel job . . . sneaky –

Collins pressed his way through the crowd surrounding King. They shook hands warmly with each other.

'Both of these promotions take effect as from December one. And let me add,' J. J. read on but very few of those present paid any attention to the bullshit about this highly significant step by the company in recognising the talent and potential of the native workforce.

When the general uproar began to subside, Collins managed to break away from his mob of well-wishers and climbed unsteadily onto the stage.

'And now,' he shouted, 'and now for the Doc's present. I'll call upon William King, Esquire, of whom it has often been said, and very truly, too. William King to the front, please.'

King mounted the platform and acknowledged the applause by turning his back to the audience and bowing deeply. Then, from behind the stage curtains, he hauled forth a large, heavily shrouded bundle.

'I'll have you know,' he said, without preamble, 'that a lot of thought and blood and sweat went into this gift for Doc. In fact . . . ' he pointed towards Collins ' . . . in one attempt, our esteemed friend and benefactor, Brian Collins, who shall be nameless, was almost laid low by the combined forces of Church and State and still bears the scars, as you can see from his lopsided walk. However,' he waved triumphantly, 'virtue prevailed in the end and so, Doc, we hope this memento will serve two purposes. We hope it will remind you of the many stimulating hours you spent in our Medical Centre and that it will also help you to keep your hand in, in case you might decide to make a comeback.'

Deftly, King whipped the cloth from the mysterious bundle and there, in all her naked glory, stood Beth, the female dummy from Limerick. But her aspect had undergone a change since her encounter with Collins. Now every visible portion of her anatomy was neatly labelled and precisely identified for Doc's future reference.

If Doc had been sober he would have lost his cool and made a fool of himself. But in his present state of insobriety he found himself joining in the raucous laughter, which was exactly the right thing to do and so the joke was no longer on him.

'Actually, Doc,' said King after a moment, 'we have something else for you.'

'Haven't you done enough?' asked Doc, gasping for breath.

King produced a portable stereo tape-recorder from behind the dummy.

'We thought,' he said, 'this yoke might come in handy when you're out collecting all that weird music.'

Doc stopped laughing.

'Come and get it,' King called and Doc wove his way to the platform to the applause of the crowd. He took possession of the recorder and began to fondle it in somewhat maudlin fashion.

'Speech,' shouted Phil Ashe again, and the crowd applauded again.

'All I can say,' said Doc, beaming mistily at them, 'is that you couldn't have picked a more acceptable gift.'

'Which one?' King asked.

'Both of them.' Doc burst out laughing or crying and trotted away to a corner, still caressing the machine.

From there the night went rapidly downhill into early morning and a good time was had by all.

Five o'clock in the morning. Malone comes rolling home. Showing great consideration, he removes his shoes and tiptoes about the flat in search of beer, knocking over whatever furniture tries to obstruct his progress. Luckily, he comes upon a bottle before he has completely demolished the flat and silence descends once again.

In his austere bedroom, King is lying on his back, watching the black rectangle of sky outside his window. A clear, frosty night full of stars. The past few weeks have seen great changes in his life. Now he is beginning to feel a heavy cloud of anticlimax enveloping him and he wishes to hell it would go away and let him go to sleep. He is on the point of joining Malone and finding himself another beer when his door flies suddenly open.

Malone's silhouette hangs in the doorway, swaying dangerously and breathing heavily through its nose.

'King,' cries Malone passionately, 'I hate your shaggin' guts!'

'My guts are as good as yours any day,' King retorts.

'How,' wails Malone, 'how can you look yourself in the face?'

'It's not easy, I admit.'

'After the way you made an eejit out of poor old Haley.'

'He didn't need any help from me,' King points out.

'Maybe he didn't,' Malone tilts over at an acute angle but saves his balance by grabbing the door frame, 'but you helped him all the same, didn't you? All the way to Taiwan, you helped him.'

'What the hell is bugging you?'

'And O'Keeffe. You screwed him rightly too, didn't you?'

King raises his head.

'What do you mean by that?' he asks sharply.

'He's the one that should have got Haley's job.' Malone tells him, 'he was the senior guy. But you screwed him good over those warped boards.'

King sits up quickly.

'Now look here, friend,' he shouts. 'Don't go blaming me for their screw-ups. What happened to them was entirely their own doing.'

Malone begins to laugh a little wildly.

'Look at you, you gobshite,' he cries. 'The smart-ass that was never going to get caught in the success trap. The genius that wouldn't let the system get hold of him. Look at you now. Promoted into Management! Jesus help us!'

'Ah, go to bed and sleep it off.'

'You're bollixed!' Malone yells. 'You know that? The shaggin' system has you by the short and curlies. And serve you shaggin' right!'

Malone begins to weep bitterly.

'You son of a bitch, King!' he cries, 'I believed in you. I really believed you could beat the system. I was sure if I tagged along with you I could beat it too.' In his distress he starts to beat his head against the door. 'Now the system has you by the knackers. You're bloody well frigged. And that means I'm bloody well frigged too. And I hate your shaggin' guts, so I do!'

Malone goes forlornly away and King pulls the blankets up about his ears and tries to get some sleep.

Up on the mountain, a fingernail moon smiles down on its perfect reflection in the lake. A rabbit screams in fear or pain. Downhill from the lake, the factory, snuggled in among the frost-polished bushes, is silent and softly glowing from the glimmer of the interior security lights, like a close encounter of the third kind.

Miss Henderson's oversized black tomcat softfoots around the grounds of the hostel in search of a morsel of rodent to satisfy his hunger or a nubile she-cat to satisfy his other appetite, or both of the above

In his mother's small cottage in Irishtown, Horny Harry' dreams are of somewhat the same nature as the cat's

Colins turns in the bed and puts his arm sleepily aroun Lucy's much expanded waist.

    – *Only another month left before the baby arrives. And then*

    – IMPURE THOUGHTS –

    – *Oh, shut up!* –

In her large comfortable empty house on the outskirts of Ballyderra, Jennifer J. Carey sits at her roll-top desk, working on the business plan for the Spanish operation. She is a chronic insomniac and takes advantage of the fact by working into the small hours. She should be home in Connecticut spending Thanksgiving with her two children and her parents, but what with the pressures of the new job . . .

Malone lies down on the couch. It doesn't seem worth while going to bed. He has just made the biggest decision of his life. No way will he let the system swallow him up like King.

'Fishing. That's the way out,' he tells himself. 'There's that seventy-five footer for sale in Dingle. With Uncle Sean in the bank and Uncle Joe in Fisheries and with the bit I've saved, I'll have no trouble getting loans and grants to buy it. Freedom! No more monthly statistical reports. No more policies. No procedures. No shagging *systems*. First thing in the morning, I'm handing in my notice. I'm out of here!'

He smiles happily and dozes off.

'Are you all right, Brian?' Lucy asks drowsily.

'Sure, sweetheart.'

'You seem a bit restless.'

'No, I'm fine.'

Lucy turns and puts her arms comfortingly around him.

'My candidate of choice,' she murmurs.

– God but you're lucky guy –

Jennifer J. Carey stretches voluptuously. How long is it since she's had the pleasure of getting into a sexy slinky dress? Too long. She thinks of her ex-husband lecturing in economics in Florida. Poor old John, a nice guy who just couldn't take the strain of her success. It would be nice to fall in love with someone again. Or even to pretend to be in love with someone. It would be nice to hear someone call her Jennifer, or even Honey, again. But all that will have to wait another while.

She takes her bottle of sleeping pills from the desk drawer and goes into the kitchen to get a glass of milk from the huge refrigerator, almost as empty as the house.

The first woman Vice-President, she thinks. Isn't that something. And you're not going to stop there either. Just keep on the way you're going. Walk that extra mile to overcome the handicap of being a woman.

She begins to undress beside the empty kingsize bed.

Yes, she tells herself, it's worth the price.

– You hope – adds the little voice inside her head.

Malone comes half awake again.

'I wonder', he asks himself, 'how much that Personnel job would pay? And a two-window office all to myself.' He squirms as the loose spring jabs into his shoulder blade. 'Maybe I'll just have another chat with Collins in the morning.'

And Ballyderra rests in peace.